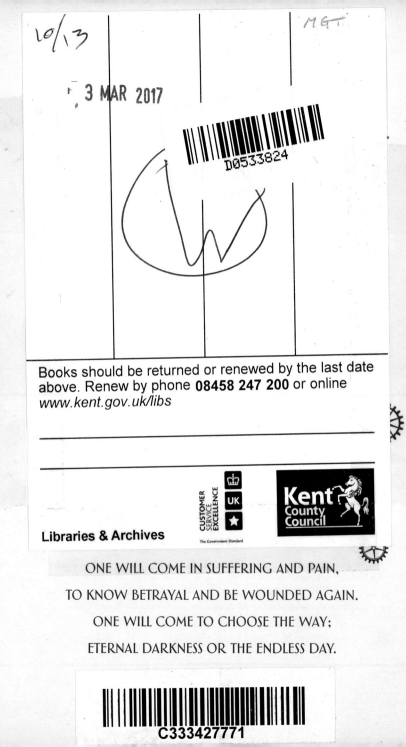

ONE WILL COME IN SUFFERING AND PAIN,

TO KNOW BETRAYAL AND BE WOUNDED AGAIN.

ONE WILL COME TO CHOOSE THE WAY;

ETERNAL DARKNESS OR THE ENDLESS DAY.

To my darling Jules,
My amazing wife, my blessing, my best friend…
This book is for you.

First published in the UK in 2013 by Usborne Publishing Ltd., Usborne House,
83-85 Saffron Hill, London EC1N 8RT, England. www.usborne.com

Text copyright © Andrew Beasley, 2013

The right of Andrew Beasley to be identified as the author of this work has been
asserted by him in accordance with the Copyright, Designs and Patents Act, 1988.

The name Usborne and the devices 🔍 🎈 are Trade Marks of
Usborne Publishing Ltd.

Cover and inside illustrations by David Wyatt. Map by Ian McNee.

A CIP catalogue record for this book is available from the British Library.

ISBN 9781409546245 JFMAMJ ASOND/13 02786/1

Printed in Reading, Berkshire, UK.

THE BATTLES OF BEN KINGDOM

THE FEAST OF RAVENS

ANDREW BEASLEY

USBORNE

CONTENTS

DAY ONE: 8TH MARCH, 1892

DAY TWO: 9TH MARCH, 1892

Day Three: 10th March, 1892

Day Four: 11th March, 1892

 # Day Five: 12th March, 1892

DAY SIX: 13TH MARCH, 1892

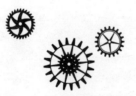

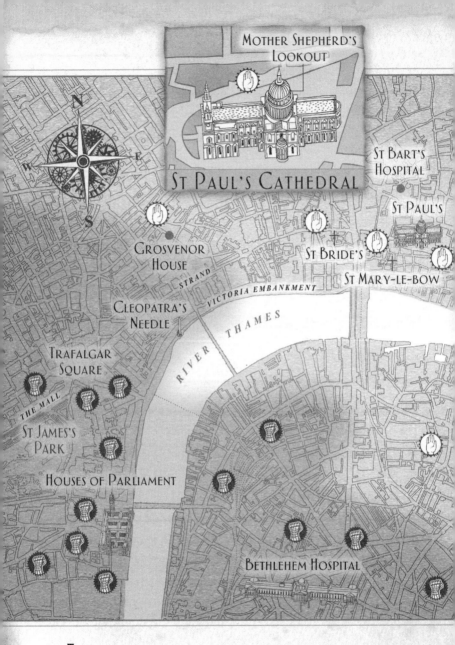

LONDON 1892

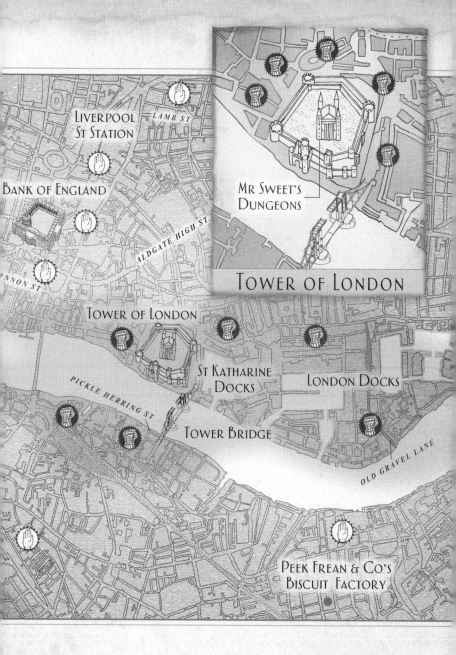

TOWER OF LONDON

LIVERPOOL
St STATION

LAMB ST

BANK OF ENGLAND

ALDGATE HIGH ST

NNON ST

MR SWEET'S
DUNGEONS

TOWER OF LONDON

TOWER OF LONDON

St KATHARINE
DOCKS

LONDON DOCKS

PICKLE HERRING ST

TOWER BRIDGE

OLD GRAVEL LANE

PEEK FREAN & CO'S
BISCUIT FACTORY

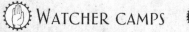 WATCHER CAMPS   LEGION TERRITORY

DAY ONE
QUEEN VICTORIA'S LONDON -
8TH MARCH, 1892

PROLOGUE

"*Ben Kingdom.*" Mr. Sweet spoke the words slowly, his voice heavy with anger; a thundercloud waiting to burst. "That boy will curse the day he crossed me."

From behind him, in the darkness of the dungeon, there came a muffled sound; the sort of noise that a panic-stricken child might make if they were bound and gagged and in the clutches of a madman.

"What was that?" Mr. Sweet asked, turning slowly. He took a pace towards his prisoner, sending cockroaches scuttling for safety. "You have something to say?"

Sweet was a bully of a man and the expensive Savile Row suit he wore did nothing to hide his muscular physique. His face was handsome in a brutal sort of way: the square jaw, the strong nose, the hard slit of a mouth beneath his luxuriant black moustache. The eyes that overflowed with fury.

It was these eyes that intimidated everyone they fell on. It seemed that no one could defy their glare; not the other members of Parliament, where Sweet served as special advisor to the Prime Minister; not the Legion, the secret army which dwelled beneath the London streets. The boy tied to the chair in front of him stood no chance.

In the flickering torchlight, Mr. Sweet watched his young captive. He smiled and the boy began to quake.

"Surely, you must agree with me," he said, his broad hand caressing his raven-black moustache. "You've lived with him, after all. Doesn't *everyone* find your brother to be a constant source of annoyance?"

A scraping sound drew Sweet's attention and he shot a glance at the other figure standing in the corner. A tall man in a battered leather coat; a man with a dinosaur claw where his right hand should have been.

Claw Carter chipped idly at the wall with his unique prosthesis, striking sparks that briefly illuminated the hollow lines of his face and the sly smile that lurked at the corner of his lips.

Carter would do well to tread carefully, thought Mr. Sweet as he returned his attentions to the boy. No one in the Legion was indispensable.

In spite of the cold in the dungeon, Sweet's prisoner, Nathaniel Kingdom, was wet with nervous sweat and Sweet could almost taste the fear that rose from the boy's pores in waves. But there was still some fight left in Nathaniel's spirit. He was not broken yet.

Mr. Sweet bent over and brought his eyes level with the boy's. Nathaniel glared back and began to curse him through the rag that had been used to silence him. Straining against the ropes that bound him to his chair, he bucked wildly, as if he were riding a savage animal; Mr. Sweet only smiled again.

"What is it with you Kingdom boys?" Sweet mocked. "You never seem to know when you're beaten."

The prisoner started to tear at his gag with his teeth, wrenching it loose with frantic twists of his head. Finally his mouth was free. "Beaten?" Nathaniel Kingdom spat. "It was my brother Ben who outwitted you!"

"Ben Kingdom", said Sweet, in a whisper somehow more threatening than his shout, "has achieved nothing. *Nothing*." His lips luxuriated over the word. "The Feast of Ravens will soon be upon us and your precious Watchers will be reduced to a stain in the footnotes of history."

"Ben stopped you getting your grubby hands on the Coin though, didn't he? He stuffed you there!"

Sweet's nostrils flared. With a snarl that was barely human, the big man swung his open hand violently towards Nathaniel's face, only to stop it a hair's breadth away. Nathaniel sat rigid in his chair, cowed and afraid.

"He has got a point," said Carter, now using the tip of his claw to pick at dirt beneath the nails of his good hand.

"How good of you to remind me, Professor Carter," said Sweet, "and how very brave. Especially considering *your* role in the whole debacle."

"It was *I* who discovered that the last remaining Judas Coin was at large," Carter protested. "It was *I* who found Ben Kingdom—"

"And it was *you* who let them both slip through your fingers," finished Sweet. "Please don't imagine that the high rank you currently hold in the Legion is something which you can rely on indefinitely. I am not a tolerant man when it comes to failure. The last Coin will be mine."

"Ben threw it into the Thames," Nathaniel continued defiantly. "You can search for it for another thousand years and you still won't find it!"

"You can believe what you like if it brings you comfort, boy," said Sweet with a snort of contempt, "but objects as evil as the Coin do not stay lost."

Sweet wasn't persuaded that the Coin lay somewhere in the silt and filth of the Thames. No, it was still at large, he was convinced of that. Hiding in some pocket or drawer or wallet, doing its work, eating its owner away from the inside.

"Wickedness calls out to wickedness," said Sweet. "The Coin *will* come to me and then the Crown of Corruption will be complete…as will my victory. All of Ben Kingdom's stupid heroics will prove to be a mere setback, an irritation to the Legion, nothing more."

A hapless cockroach scurried across the stone floor, its antennae twitching in happy ignorance. Sweet crushed it beneath his foot, and Nathaniel couldn't stop himself from flinching as he heard the crunch that marked its death.

"Life can be so fragile," said Sweet. "Believe me, it would have been better for Ben Kingdom if he had stayed in the gutter where he belongs."

"He's not afraid of you," said Nathaniel.

"But you are, aren't you?" Mr. Sweet goaded. "I always knew that you were the one with the brains."

Nathaniel saw the bottomless hatred in Sweet's eyes and the last of his bravado shrivelled to ashes in his mouth. "Are you going to kill me?"

"Oh no," Sweet laughed. "You're worth much more to

me alive. You are bait, don't you see? Something I can use to lure your brother into my clutches. However..." And here he paused, enjoying the moment. "There is an experiment that you can help me with in the meantime. The Legion have a new weapon, but as yet it is untested. Professor Carter, would you do the honours?"

Nathaniel watched mutely as Claw Carter walked to the other end of the cell. For the first time, Nathaniel's eyes made out another door in the darkness, and a shot of terror ran through him. There was something about that door that was very wrong. It was made from sturdy wooden planks, criss-crossed with iron bands. Long deadbolts secured it top and bottom, and as Sweet drew them slowly back Nathaniel felt all the hairs stand upright on his arms. The door was only three feet tall.

What the heck was in there?

The door swung wide and opened onto utter darkness.

There was a moment of agonizing stillness.

"I want you to meet a friend of mine," said Mr. Sweet. "He has a gift for the whole of London and I'd like you to be the first one to enjoy his...talents."

As Nathaniel's eyes strained to pierce the darkness, he saw a shadow detach itself from the inky black. Claw Carter moved aside and allowed a diminutive figure to step out through the door. Carter's long face split into a wolfish grin. "Permit me to introduce you to the Nightmare Child."

At first, Nathaniel thought that it was just a boy, an odd, almost awkward child with chubby cheeks and pale hair in ringlets. Then, as he watched, it opened its mouth wide, as if it had been told to take a spoonful of medicine. There was a cracking sound and the Nightmare Child's mouth opened wider still, until it became a gaping maw.

Nathaniel watched in appalled silence as a stream of fog began to pour from the Child's mouth and fill the room like rising water. Nathaniel shuddered as the wave reached him and pooled around his feet. As if on command, the fog began to tease at Nathaniel's legs, growing long white fingers that climbed up his body like a spider.

Help me! Nathaniel screamed inside his head. *HELP ME, BEN!*

"Oh, don't worry," said Sweet, as if reading Nathaniel's mind. "I'm counting on your brother coming for you. And when he does, oh what a welcome I have planned for him."

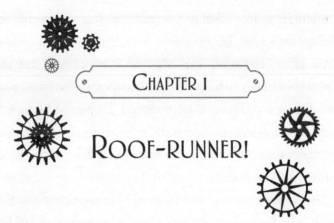

CHAPTER 1

ROOF-RUNNER!

"Benjamin Kingdom! Prepare to defend yourself!"

Ben was trapped, and he knew it.

He quickly cast his eyes around, searching for the source of the voice. To his left he saw chimney pots rising up out of a sea of coal dust and ashes. To his right, more chimneys, more choking fumes. Overhead lay a filthy blanket of cloud, and below, three storeys down, lay the cobbled streets. It was a view of London that few were familiar with, but it was as normal as breathing to Ben.

At the very edge of his vision, Ben thought he caught a phantom of movement, a shape that appeared momentarily from behind a ramshackle stack only to disappear again, leaving just a stirring in the smoke. Without any thought of the danger, Ben pelted along the ridge of a roof, his feet finding purchase at lightning speed, like a tightrope walker at the climax of his act. It was not the easiest escape path, even at the best of times, but for the last ten weeks of his young life, none of his options had been easy.

Too soon, however, Ben ran out of roof and his feet came stammering to a halt. A tile snapped beneath his weight and slid away into empty space, almost taking him with it. Ben felt the strong hands of gravity reaching for him, doing their best to steal his balance. Instinctively, he grabbed hold of a chimney pot to steady himself while he fought to regain his footing – and not for the first time he was grateful for his skyboots with their studded rubber soles, part of the Watcher uniform he wore.

When his feet were secure again, Ben paused on the edge of the drop, his heart a racing engine. He lifted his brass-rimmed goggles from his eyes and considered his options. Through the haze spewing from factory chimneys and ten thousand household hearths, Ben could make out the ghosts of church steeples and the great dome of St Paul's, rising up from the patchwork acres of rooftops. Beneath him were the streets of London, waiting to welcome him with an embrace of broken bones. And behind him, somewhere, was his pursuer.

Ben hesitated, uncertain which way to turn. *Come on, Benny boy*, he urged himself. He had to move and move fast, he knew that much. His hunter was not far behind and past experience suggested that he shouldn't expect things to go easily. Adrenaline surged through his body, making Ben feel vibrant and alive. He was a Watcher, after all; part of a secret army, hiding and surviving on the rooftops of the city: he didn't scare easily.

Three months ago, Ben would have laughed at the idea that he had any sort of destiny beyond scratching out a meagre living as best he could. But then three months ago he had been totally ignorant of a lot of things. Such as the battle that had been raging for centuries, with the Watchers on one side and the Legion on the other. The Watchers in the high places and the Legion in their network of tunnels. The Above and the Under. Good and evil. Opposite, but not equal.

Ben knew about the war now. And his own part in it.

He faltered, uncertain which way to turn, and the words of his mentor, Mr. Moon, sprang to mind. *Stop larking about and focus!*

Jago Moon was a man with many hidden talents, steeped in the knowledge and law of the Watchers. He was a master swordsman, which came as a surprise to people who assumed (as Moon intended them to) that he was a slightly insane bookseller. But that was only the beginning of Moon's gifts. The old man's hearing was so acute that he didn't even need to use his eyes when he was sword fighting. Of course, the old boy didn't have much choice on that score; he was blind as a bat and twice as scary.

Ben did his best to imitate Moon now, using all of his senses to prepare himself for fight or flight. *You never know when you might not have eyes to help you*, Moon had advised him. Moon was full of cheery thoughts like that.

Fighting against the hubbub of the city, Ben listened for sounds that he could use to pinpoint his position. He had always considered himself to be the king of the streets, but learning to navigate across the rooftops was almost like starting from scratch. He closed his eyes, shut out all the distractions and concentrated.

A scream: the angry friction of metal against metal. *Brakes*, Ben recognized immediately. *A hiss of steam. The constant rumble of iron wheels.* He breathed in and tasted the sharp tang of coal dust in the air. *So, I'm near a station. What else?*

Above the drone of other voices, Ben could make out the barking of costermongers trying to outdo each other as they drummed up trade. He pieced the details together, picturing the map of London in his mind. *A railway station near a market? That would be Liverpool Street*, he realized with some satisfaction. *So that would mean I'm on…Lamb Street. Probably.*

He opened his eyes and looked around for some confirmation. As the sea of smoke shifted, he made out that Spitalfields Market *was* dead ahead. Ben sniffed the air, drawing in the organic rot of vegetables. *Nice.* The problem now was whether he could make the jump.

"Arm yourself, Ben Kingdom!" boomed his hunter. "Get ready to fight like a man of destiny."

Ben still couldn't pinpoint where the voice was coming from, but it was undoubtedly closer than before. One thing was for certain – he needed to get onto a flat roof if he was going to stand a chance in one-to-one combat. And by his calculations, the flat roof of the market was less than eight feet away. *Well, maybe nine or ten*, Ben admitted. *Certainly not more than twelve.*

The Watchers were faced with these challenges every day of the week and had devised numerous ingenious methods to help them bridge the gap between one building and another. Ladders, planks, zip wires and ropes were all stashed at strategic locations. Unfortunately for Ben, this particular junction wasn't one of them.

"I'm coming!" said the pursuer, from somewhere too close for comfort.

"I'm going," said Ben, and he took three careful steps backwards, enough to give him a short run-up. Pushing down with his legs and swinging powerfully upwards with his arms, Ben fixed his sight firmly on the opposite roof and launched himself into the air towards it. *No more than twelve feet*, he told himself as the air rushed around him. *I can do this!* And even as he thought it, Ben knew that he was dropping too fast. The arc of his leap had been too shallow. *Of course I could be wrong*, thought Ben, too late. *It might be more like fifteen feet, in which case I'm absolutely stuffed.*

Spitalfields *was* further away than he had anticipated and Ben's heart was in his mouth as his feet fell short and the wall loomed up in front of him. He threw up his arms as his body slammed painfully against the brickwork, punching all the air from his lungs. Scrabbling madly, his fingers managed to get a grip on the guttering. Then he hung there for a moment, as helpless as a rabbit in a butcher's shop window.

Gritting his teeth against the pain, Ben heaved himself up, first getting one elbow up onto the roof, then the other, and finally his whole bruised body.

"Easy," he said, with a lopsided grin. "Jago Moon would be proud of me."

Then the quarterstaff struck him from behind, catching him in the crook of his knees and sweeping his legs out from underneath him. *Or maybe not.*

Ben's eyes blazed as he saw his assailant for the first time.

"You fancy playing rough, eh?" Ben taunted, but the words had barely passed his lips when a missile caught him low in the gut, leaving him gasping for breath. It was a crossbow bolt with a weighted head, fired at close range by his slender attacker, who was now backflipping away across the roof.

He rubbed his bruised stomach, grateful that the bolt that had hit him was made for stunning a foe, not killing them. His eyes locked on his attacker. Ben had fought with this opponent many times before, and there was something almost teasing about their manner which made Ben see red.

And then it came: the tinkling laugh.

"So it's like that, is it?" said Ben, reaching for his belt and unclipping a short brass tube. With a practised flick of the wrist it expanded into a quarterstaff of his own, which he spun from hand to hand; another of the skills that Jago Moon had taught him.

He knew that his assailant was not alone. When they came for him like this, they always hunted in pairs, and the deep voice that had called out to him certainly did not belong to the slight, loose-limbed creature who remained teasingly out of reach. Ben braced himself and waited for the thud of feet on tiles that would announce their arrival.

Ben strained his ears. No sound came.

He looked around him, keeping light on his feet, waiting and alert. Then he heard it. It was a sound which still gave him goosebumps. The ugly clouds parted and swirled into eddies, stirred by the beating of enormous wings.

"Look no further," said the angel who landed in front of him. "And draw your sword."

"Here we go again," said Ben.

Even though this was by no means the first time that he had encountered an angel, Ben could not completely control the quiver of fear which suddenly grabbed him. There was something deeply unnerving about facing a being that was not of this world.

The angel in front of him was tall and powerful, with long dark hair hanging around a face which was simultaneously young and incredibly old. It was as if this man in the prime of his life had somehow witnessed everything that was terrible throughout history; all his scars were on the inside. He was wearing an open-necked, high-collared shirt, and a long, black, square-tailed coat, which had been tailored for him personally to make allowance for the huge white wings which emerged from beneath it.

What always rattled Ben though, even more than the viciously sharp sword that the angel had drawn from its scabbard, were the angel's eyes. They didn't just see him, they saw *into* him. Everything that he was, everything that he had done, no secret was left undisturbed. It was a terrible thing, Ben thought, to be seen by an angel.

With a calmness born out of practice, Ben retracted his quarterstaff using the button on its hilt and clipped it back onto his belt. Then slowly, his gaze not flinching from the angel's weapon, Ben reached over his shoulder and drew his own sword from its sheath on his back. It was a light blade, slender and finely balanced. It was, as Jago Moon had been keen to instil, a weapon of defence and last resort. To take a life, even the life of an enemy, was not the Watcher way.

Ben flicked his wrist, making the tip of his sword carve invisible curls in the air.

The angel smiled approvingly and then unleashed his attack.

Ben didn't have time to think any more; all he could do was react.

The angel's sword slashed towards him in a furious

barrage of blows; right cheek; left flank; right flank; left cheek. Ben blocked every swipe but he felt himself being forced backwards across the roof, step by step. Desperately he made a counter-attack, diving forwards and then rolling back up to his feet behind the angel, with a spinning slash at his opponent's legs. However, a single beat of his wings lifted the angel above the arc of Ben's blade, and when he landed he attacked with renewed ferocity, sending Ben scurrying back on his hands and feet just to stay out of reach of the onslaught.

Ben tried to concentrate on what Jago Moon had taught him. *Focus. Breathe. Anticipate,* Moon would say. *Choices and consequences, Ben.* All good advice, he was sure, but pretty hard to manage when someone was trying to hack your head off.

Ben scrabbled back onto his feet just in time to parry an almighty downward blow which would have cleaved his head in two. His body still ached where he had slammed into the wall, and his arms were getting heavier, his muscles burning. Ben was losing and the angel knew it.

It was then that he backed into his other opponent, who had been waiting patiently on the rooftop. While he had been focusing on not getting his bonce chopped off, Ben had forgotten about the other attacker, the one with the crossbow and the playful laugh. Too late he felt their arms around him and, caught off balance, he was flung to the floor. The small figure followed through with a sharp open-handed blow to his wrist, knocking Ben's sword from his hand, before pinning him securely to the ground.

Ben lay on his back, struggling for breath, while his adversary sat astride his chest, knees on his shoulders, hands clamped firmly around his wrists. He looked for his sword. It was only a few feet away. It may as well have been miles.

He looked up into the face of his victor.

And, as always, she laughed.

"We must stop meeting like this," said Lucy Lambert, her cheeks flushed with effort.

"Very funny," said Ben, meaning to sound rather nonchalant about the whole thing but coming across as more petulant than he would have liked. "You can let me up now. I've had enough training for one day, don't you think?"

"Anything you say, oh mighty one," said Lucy, releasing him. She put out her hand and pulled Ben to his feet. He flashed her a quick grin but Lucy only held his gaze for a moment before turning away. She busied herself tidying her equipment and checking everything was in place on her belt.

She was a strong girl, in more ways than one, Ben knew. She was a Watcher to the core, standing there in the leather trench coat they all wore, her brass-rimmed goggles on the top of her head, like a crown in her long honey-coloured hair. Instinctively her hand went to her face as she felt his eyes on her, touching the long livid scar that split her right cheek in two and the eyepatch which hid the worst of her old wound.

"Be good," she said out of the side of her mouth. "Josiah is coming. None of your backchat."

The angel approached them, his footsteps measured. "Well," said Josiah, slipping his sword back into its sheath. "How do you think that went?"

"Sweet as a nut," said Ben.

"Apart from the fact that you would have been killed if I were Claw Carter or one of the Legion's Feathered Men," Josiah replied.

"All right," Ben snapped. "Keep your halo on."

Ben was tired, he was bleeding from grazes to his knees and elbows, and his head was spinning. Since he had joined the Watchers, most days had followed the same pattern. Endless training, constant lectures from Jago Moon and Mother Shepherd, the ageing leader of the Watchers. *Think like this. Act like that. Be prepared.* And yet, according to them, he still wasn't ready to go on anything more challenging than a long-range scouting mission. All he ever got was *Not yet. Not today. When the time is right.* It was driving him mad with frustration.

The sense of elation that he had felt just moments earlier when he was jumping free, suddenly abandoned him, and the weight of his responsibility chained him to the spot. Ben felt Josiah looking at him, those ancient eyes stripping away all his outer layers of protection to bore into his soul.

The Watchers believed that Ben was the Hand of Heaven, the great leader promised by prophecy. It was a great destiny, but not one that Ben had asked for.

Deep down, Ben couldn't help but wonder if they had got it all wrong.

Did it seem likely that a street urchin from the East End, always in some sort of trouble, was really the one person who would end the war between the Watchers and the Legion? Ben was always up for a dare, but even he wouldn't have picked himself for this one. Mother Shepherd certainly had the wisdom, Jago Moon had the courage, and Lucy Lambert had just about all the qualities necessary, as far as he could see. But him? Ben Kingdom from Old Gravel Lane?

And what if he let them down? What then?

Ben rolled his shoulders and pinched at an imaginary

pain in his neck. *Head up, Benny boy*, he told himself. *Put on a brave face. Brass it out.*

Ben retrieved his own sword. He could see Josiah and Lucy waiting for him, before they all returned to camp. They looked at him with expressions full of expectation, but Ben was certain that his own doubts were written all over his face.

"I'll catch you up," said Ben, dropping down on one knee to fiddle with a shoelace that didn't need tying. "If Nathaniel is back yet," he called to Lucy, "give him a dead arm from me."

"I'll do better than that," laughed Lucy. "I'll tell him how his little brother was beaten by a girl...again!"

"Thanks for that," said Ben as he watched them leave.

That was another thing Ben found annoying. His big brother was allowed out on proper missions, and had even been in a few skirmishes, but Ben – the leader-in-waiting, so Mother Shepherd said – was never even allowed out of eyeshot.

"Give me strength," Ben whispered softly, his hand dipping into his pocket and touching an old silver Coin which lay there. "Or failing that, give me a bit of luck."

CHAPTER 2

THE CAPTAIN'S ORDERS

Captain Mickelwhite enjoyed his status in the Legion. His father was the Duke of Gloucester, and there was a title and an inheritance waiting for Mickelwhite, should he ever choose to return to the family home. But the truth was that money and status were not enough for him. As a young child he had always enjoyed hurting animals, and as a boy at boarding school he'd found there was fun to be had hurting other children too. He had told the headmaster it had been an accident when the other boy lost his legs but, of course, that had been a lie.

Mickelwhite remembered the day well. He often revisited it and replayed those formative moments. The headmaster had been afraid of him; Mickelwhite had seen it in the bead of sweat that trickled from his thinning hairline and the relief on his face when he told Mickelwhite that he was expelled. His father could easily have covered up the whole messy affair – dukes were good at things like that – but Mickelwhite had had a glimpse of his future on that day. The fear in the headmaster's eyes had been simply exquisite. And being in the Legion meant that he got to taste others' fear every single day.

The Legion had a way of rewarding those with his particular set of skills. Knight Commander Claw Carter had recognized his leadership potential immediately. Indeed, fourteen years old and already a captain, Mickelwhite would have said that he was Carter's favourite – or at least he had been, until Ben Kingdom had come along. It was particularly irksome to Mickelwhite that an arrogant East End street rat like Kingdom should be the focus of such attention. Carter seemed to believe that Kingdom was some sort of "chosen one". *What rot!* It was certainly a pleasing twist that Kingdom had been instrumental in Carter's fall from glory.

Since then, Mickelwhite had done his best to distance himself from Carter and had quickly found himself a new sponsor within the Legion: Mr. Sweet himself. Now there was a man who Mickelwhite *did* admire. Carter was a spent force, but Mr. Sweet was a member of the Council of Seven, the ultimate power in the Legion. That was why Mickelwhite was standing guard outside a dungeon door in the heart of the Under; Mr. Sweet had ordered it.

Mickelwhite heard footsteps approaching – solid, confident steps – and knew immediately that they belonged to Mr. Sweet. He squared his shoulders and lifted his head.

The great man came to a halt and Mickelwhite saluted him the Legion way, bringing his left fist up to his chest with a thump.

"Mr. Sweet, sir," said Mickelwhite, his voice cracking slightly in Sweet's powerful presence. "At your command."

"I know, boy," said Sweet, his voice low. "I am going inside now to prepare…a special treat, shall we say. In five minutes' time I shall be receiving guests and you are to let them in and lock the door behind them. However –" and here Sweet raised a finger in warning – "once all of my visitors are inside you are not, on any account, to unlock this door until I order you to do so. Do you understand?"

"Yes, sir!"

"Do not weaken on me, boy," Sweet emphasized. "Even if there is a monstrous ballyhoo, even if you hear begging or screaming or mewling, or are promised

extravagant bribes, no one walks out of this room...
Except me!"

Captain Mickelwhite waited eagerly for the prisoners
to arrive. *More Watcher scum*, he thought. *Preferably Ben
Kingdom*. So he was taken completely by surprise when a
strange party turned the corner and approached his post.
Mickelwhite made the Legion salute and stood stock-still
while they trooped silently into the room.

One by one they passed him: a tall woman in a raven-
feather hood, her face all shadows; a shrunken dwarf;
a man of enormous obesity; a thin foppish man with long
manicured nails; a woman dressed in flowing green silk,
her eyes unnaturally wide; a dried husk of a man, with
long limbs hanging loosely over the edges of a bath chair,
wheeled along by a solemn servant. They didn't
acknowledge Mickelwhite and he made no attempt to
catch their gaze; for they were the Council of Seven. Their
rule in the Legion was unquestioned. Their power was to
be feared.

Mickelwhite stayed motionless by the door until they
were all inside. He felt thrilled to have seen all of the
Council of Seven. How many others in the Legion could
make that boast? he wondered.

As ordered, once they were all inside Mickelwhite took
the key from his pocket. His fingers trembled slightly as

he turned the key in the lock and the bolt snapped into place. His curiosity getting the better of him, he began to imagine what sort of treat Mr. Sweet could possibly have in store for the rest of the Council.

Then he heard the gasps. And the cries. And the blood-curdling screams.

Mickelwhite changed his mind and tried to keep his imagination locked as tightly as that door.

What could possibly be evil enough to frighten the Legion's most terrifying members? What sort of monster could scare them to death?

CHAPTER 3

A WORK OF EVIL

As a weary sun gave up the battle of the day, Ben made his way across the Watcher encampment. It was a nomadic life in the Watchers, always on the move, never stopping on the same rooftop for more than one night. Every day Mother Shepherd decided on a new location for their camp, and then the work began in earnest.

Lookouts had to be posted, perimeters guarded, quick escape paths planned, with rope ladders and bridge planks put in place. Then the tents had to be set up – the canvas and tarpaulin awnings that they fixed into the sheltered lee of any available wall. Then the waterproof groundsheets were laid and the bedding rolls prepared.

Fires were lit, for cooking, cleaning and washing, and coal and wood found to keep them burning. Then came the hunt for food. Usually it was a mix of whatever vegetables they were able to get their hands on, some meat if they were lucky, a crust of bread if not. But no hungry belly ever went unfed. It was one of the things that Ben most admired about their secret society – everyone was welcome: beggars and princes, sinners and saints.

As tired as he was, Ben still had the energy to smile. Up here, under the sky, he had discovered a reassuring homeliness that had somehow always been absent from the cold, damp room his family used to live in. It was a mother's touch that had been missing, Ben recognized with a sharp stab of regret.

Ben now knew that his father, Jonas, and elder brother, Nathaniel, didn't blame him for the death of the woman who should have bound them all together. It wasn't Ben's fault that his mother lost her life bringing him into the world. But the wound that had been left was deep and they all felt it still.

Ben passed groups of Watchers gathered in intimate circles around their fires. Some of them raised their hands to him in a wave or a salute, and Ben nodded in return.

Part of Ben wished that he could just be an ordinary

Watcher, rather than the chosen boy who would supposedly lead them to victory one day. As it was, he was set apart. Loved, but only from afar. Too special, too different, to just sit and share a bowl of stew.

Mother Shepherd had taught him the prophecy, until he knew it line by line.

One will come to lead the fight,
To defeat the darkness, bring the triumph of the light.
One will come with fire as his crown,
To bring the Legion tumbling down...

In truth, the only part Ben thought sounded really like him was the "fire as his crown" part. The Watchers were waiting for a hero with red hair. He could argue about a lot of things, but he couldn't deny being ginger. Apparently, being the chosen one meant that Ben had one crucial responsibility; he had to choose between the powers of evil and good, what the prophecy referred to as "eternal darkness" or "endless day".

At first, that didn't seem like such a bad lot. Whichever side he chose would win, so choose the Watchers, they win, end of story.

Only it wasn't as simple as that, because *every* one of Ben's choices could upset the balance. He was with the Watchers now, and they accepted him as the Hand of Heaven, but if he slipped, if he did the wrong thing in the wrong place at the wrong time, then he could just as easily become the Hand of Hell and the saviour of the Legion.

How's that for pressure?

The Watchers all spoke about him with great respect. Around the cooking fires they told of how he had parted the clouds and caused hailstones the size of marbles to smash the Feathered Men from the sky. In excited whispers, they related the moment he had brought his own father back from death. The glorious time when Ben was used as the Hand of Heaven, and power flowed *through* him, knitting Jonas Kingdom's body back together again, and putting a fresh beat in his still heart. Ben remembered it too. The problem was that he didn't recall it in the same way.

His hand *did* throb when he was under intense pressure, but what did that prove? And anyway, it seemed to be happening less and less. It *had* hailed that day, and the hail was heavy and it did drive the Feathered Men back, but how could Ben say for certain that the hail had fallen because *he* had wanted it to?

What had happened to his father was definitely a miracle – Claw Carter had slit him open and there'd been no doubt that the wound was fatal. However, whose miracle was it? Ben remembered placing his right hand on his father's chest and the wound closing up beneath his fingers, but Josiah the angel had been beside him and *his* hand had lain on top of Ben's.

Didn't it make more sense that Josiah was the healer? Wasn't it more likely to be the angel than the street urchin? And yet all the Watchers, Mother Shepherd especially, were convinced that it was Ben.

He scanned the grubby faces around him, longing to find his brother and the comfort of his presence. It shouldn't take this long to get to the docks and back... unless something had gone badly wrong.

Come on, Nathaniel. You should have been back ages ago. All you had to do was go and find some more rope.

The night was descending and it was a dangerous thing to be a Watcher alone in the darkness.

Ben was on the point of heading back out across the city to search for his brother when he saw Mother Shepherd beckoning him. There was no greater honour than to be invited to sit down and eat with the leader of the Watchers, and yet Ben felt the heaviness in his feet. Mother Shepherd had such faith in him; Ben just hoped that he wouldn't let her down.

"Benjamin, my dear boy," she said as he drew near. She was an old woman, but in spite of the game that the years had played on her skin and hair, her sight was still sharp and her mind was young and vital. The light from the fire lit up her face, illuminating a myriad of lines, but when her eyes met Ben's, all those years seemed to drop away.

"Have you seen Nathaniel?" Ben asked hopefully.

"He's a little late returning from his solo scavenging mission, but I don't think we need to get too worried yet. He wasn't going anywhere dangerous," she said gently. "Your father is following his route, just to be on the safe side. Here," she went on, "I've saved you a seat."

Gratefully, Ben positioned himself close to the flames, rubbing some heat back into his cold knees. Mother Shepherd took her own shawl and wrapped it round his shoulders. "This should keep out the chill," she said. Ben received it without protest. Mother Shepherd would warm the world if she could.

Jago Moon was there too, slurping noisily at a dish of steaming tea. He grinned at Ben, his blind white eyes rolling as ceaselessly as the sea. Sitting silently beside Mr. Moon was Ghost. *See no evil, speak no evil*, thought Ben; Moon blind, Ghost mute.

Ghost remained an enigma amongst the Watchers. Ben had found that everyone here had a tale to tell, but Ghost's story could only be guessed at. He was a year or two older than Ben, strong in body and spirit. His head was shaven and his skin was the deep black-brown of mahogany.

44

But the rest of his life was a mystery – Ghost had never spoken a word.

Molly Marbank was there too. She was a tiny young girl, hardly more than six, one of the many orphans who the Watchers had rescued from the streets. She had been as thin as a stick when Josiah found her; now there was more meat on her bones and a brightness to her eyes. Josiah, the mighty angel, was seated patiently beside her, watching with confusion as the little girl wrapped a length of wool around his outstretched fingers.

"No, silly," laughed Molly, "you're doing it all wrong. Let me show you."

It was an incredible sight, Ben thought – an angel playing cat's cradle.

"Wipe that look off your face," said Moon, cuffing his lips on his sleeve. "I can hear your silly smile from here." Ben didn't stop grinning though, and he recognized the affection in Moon's voice. They sat together, dipping hunks of bread into bowls of hearty stew; a happy communion of slurping and burping.

"So," said Ben, as they settled down contently. "How's the work going on the Liberator?"

"Good, good," said Mother Shepherd. She smiled broadly and placed her hand on his. "It was such a wonderful idea of yours."

Ben beamed from the compliment. He saw himself as more of a "doer" than a "thinker", and the Liberator would certainly allow the Watchers to do some really good "doing".

His father was in charge of the team that was building it, and Ben had never felt more proud of his pa. In the past, before they joined the Watchers, there had been a distance between them that neither of them knew how to bridge, but the Liberator project was bringing them closer than ever before.

"It's going to be an incredible weapon when it's finished," said Ben with a whistle.

"Is that what you think we need then?" growled Moon. "A weapon? Think we can't handle ourselves?"

"Don't jump on him," Mother Shepherd intervened. "Give Ben a moment to explain."

Ben fished for the words. "Well, we're at war, aren't we? Don't you need weapons to win a war?"

"And what do you think the Watchers' greatest weapon is?" asked Mother Shepherd.

Ben hesitated while the others looked on, waiting for his reply. It was so often like this; everyone expecting him to live up to his new status as the Hand of Heaven.

"Weapon…" Ben repeated, playing for time. Although the Watchers were a fighting force, their credo was one of self-defence – despite the fact that they all knew one day that would have to change. The Legion were intent on wiping the Watchers out – that was not a problem that could be turned away with kind words and a cup of tea.

Ben wracked his brain… Did Mother Shepherd want him to say "The Liberator"? Ben had seen his father working on it earlier, using his skilled hands to smooth the wood, directing others to fashion the pipes. It was certainly going to be a thing of beauty. But no, Ben decided, Mother Shepherd was looking for a different answer.

Quarterstaffs? Crossbows? Surprise?

"Courage," said Ben, when the expectant silence grew too heavy for him to bear. Then, hedging his bets, he added, "And swords."

Mother Shepherd laughed then, though not unkindly. "I do love you, Ben," she said. "But no. Our most powerful weapon is forgiveness."

Ben looked bewildered. "How are we going to destroy the Legion with that?"

"We want to defeat them, Ben, not destroy them. There is a difference."

"I don't get it."

"The Legion won't rest until every one of us is dead; it is their desire to *destroy* us."

"So we do them, before they do us," said Ben. "Isn't that the plan?"

"No, Ben," Mother Shepherd explained, "we want to stop the Legion, not kill Legionnaires."

"So what do you suggest when I come up against Claw Carter again? Harsh language?" Ben could feel his frustration slipping over into anger.

"Most of the Legionnaires are not evil, Ben. They are bitter and angry and full of resentment, but they are not inherently evil."

"I must remember that the next time they're trying to kill me," snapped Ben.

Mother Shepherd continued in her same patient tone. "Forgiveness is powerful, Ben, never underestimate it. Forgiveness can change a person from the inside out; set their whole life down a different path." She smiled at him gently. "You know the Watcher Creed." She began to recite:

"Love makes us wise.

Tears make us strong.

Patience makes us steadfast.

Justice makes us humble.

Forgiveness will bring us victory."

Ben listened in silence; he had heard this all before. Nice sentiments, but kind words won't butter no parsnips, as the saying went.

Mother Shepherd looked at him; an intent and penetrating gaze. "You know that I forgive you, don't you, Benjamin?"

"What have I done now?" said Ben.

Mother Shepherd didn't rise to the bait. "I will always forgive you, Ben. No matter what."

Ben got up, irritated and confused, not wanting to hear any more of this. *I'm doing my best. Isn't that ever enough?*

"I'm tired," he said. "I'm going to turn in now, if that's all right with you."

He didn't wait for an answer and sloped away with his hands deep in his pockets. As always, he felt a coin there. *The* Coin. He had tricked everybody into thinking that he had thrown it into the Thames. Mother Shepherd couldn't know that he still had it, could she? He touched the silver and felt a familiar shiver run through him. The Coin was his guilty little secret, the one part of him that he had managed to keep private.

When it first came into his possession – no, he corrected himself, when he *stole* it from his father – he had assumed that it was a valuable piece of Roman silver; a coin of archaeological interest and worth a bob or two. However, he had come to learn that it was infinitely more valuable from that.

The thirty Judas Coins were imbued with temptation,

each one of them having the power to strip a man down to his most brutal desires. But the last one, the thirtieth, the Coin which Ben held now, was something more than that.

In the battle that had been raging for two thousand years between the Legion and the Watchers, this last Coin could prove to be the tipping point.

More potent. More powerful.

The final missing component of the Crown of Corruption, the wearer of which, the Legion believed, would be able to bend all men to their will.

Ben stalked over to the edge of the roof. He clutched the Coin in his fist and his emotions became cloudy as it exerted its dark pull. He took his left hand from his pocket and examined the Legion mark that was branded on his palm. He hated to see it; a symbol of evil which he had allowed to be burned into his flesh. Just another of his stupid mistakes; a constant reminder of why Mother Shepherd and all the other Watchers must be wrong about him. Would their great leader *really* be a boy like him?

It reminded him of something else too – the promise from the Legion that he could lead *them* to victory instead.

His head began to spin with conflicting emotions. Behind him, the others were laughing and he felt a sudden flash of anger. *They'd better not be laughing at me.* If the

Watchers were going to laugh at him, why shouldn't he
go back to the Legion? They didn't muck around with
nonsense about forgiveness. The Legion knew how to
fight. They wanted him to be the Hand of Hell. The
Legion—

Something on the horizon caught Ben's attention then,
and as his focus shifted he felt disorientated, almost sick
from the turmoil in his mind. He released the Coin inside
his pocket, as if it were a hot coal, breaking his connection
with its dark influence. He was left feeling drained and
somehow hollowed out, as if everything that was good in
him had been sucked dry.

Taking a second to regain his senses, Ben tried to make
sense of what he was witnessing.

"Quickly!" He motioned to the others. "You need to see
this!"

Hearing the urgency in his tone, they ran over and
joined him in gazing across the city; Ben, Lucy, Ghost, Jago
Moon, Mother Shepherd, Molly Marbank and Josiah, the
wool still threaded through his fingers.

"I don't understand," said Lucy. Ben had never heard
anything except strength in her voice and so the tremor in
her words sent a shiver down his spine.

As they watched, a mist was rising over to the west,
dense and unearthly. From its pulsating dome, long white

tentacles of fog emerged and began teasing and worming their way down alleys and side streets. Searching. Tasting…

Like every Londoner, Ben knew a thing or two about fog. The city was famous across the globe for its "pea-soupers" – the poisonous green clouds of mist and soot that regularly flooded the streets. They weren't always green either. Ben had seen them sickly yellow with phosphor near the match factories and ugly brown down by the tanneries. Either way, the smog was a curse on the East End, a fog so thick and fetid that it could clog your lungs and choke you dead. But as fearful and terrible as that was, Ben knew that somehow what he was seeing was worse.

This fog was alive. That was the only way Ben could describe it.

Natural fog didn't stop at the rooftops. Natural fog didn't move like the jellyfish Ben had seen in the Carnival of Curiosities when it came to Hampstead Heath. This fog seemed to have purpose, a plan. It was like some vast sea creature that had been washed ashore by a strange tide. And his brother and father were out there somewhere…

"Will someone please tell me what you're all staring at," demanded Moon, bristling with irritation.

Mother Shepherd took a step closer to him so that they were standing shoulder to shoulder, and her hand took his.

"A work of evil," she said.

CHAPTER 4

FUN AND GAMES

The creature was called the Nightmare Child for good reason.

Like his cousins, the Feathered Men, he had been an angel – a cherub in fact – until he had been exiled. Now the only thing he shared with the heavenly cherubim was his childlike stature and curls of golden hair. But he was not a child. He was ancient and terrible, and his greatest pleasure was to reveal to mere mortals the deepest fears of their souls.

The Nightmare Child skipped through the fog.

That was not his name, of course. But it would do very nicely for now.

He was having such fun.

In a low tenement in the Old Nichol, he treated one family to a delightful game of charades. Without using a single word, he showed them his best impersonations of loved ones who had passed away. They enjoyed it so much that they ran shouting down the street to tell their neighbours all about it.

In one grand house in Knightsbridge he stood very quietly in the corner with his hands over his eyes. When the owner of the property tremulously asked him what he was doing, the Nightmare Child replied, "Playing hide-and-seek. I'm going to count to ten and then come looking for you. One. Two. Three…" There had been no need to get to ten.

Such fun. Such games.

And he was just getting started.

DAY TWO
9TH MARCH, 1892

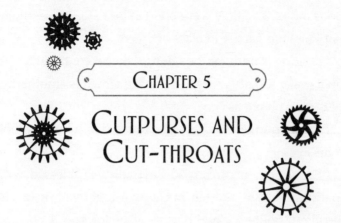

CHAPTER 5

CUTPURSES AND CUT-THROATS

"This is the awakening of a new age." Mr. Sweet's voice filled the sanctuary at the heart of the Under like a violent storm. "A glorious new age for the Legion!"

Captain Mickelwhite stood amid the massed ranks of Legionnaires in the dark cathedral and shouted his approval. At Mickelwhite's side stood John Bedlam, his brother-in-arms. They were quite different in most respects. Mickelwhite had white-blond hair and an aristocratic expression of absolute contempt. Bedlam was a squat little thug from some back alley, with a boxer's flattened nose. But the Legion united them. With a thousand others, they were bonded by hate, a resentment that knew no barrier of class or creed.

"London is ours for the taking," Sweet continued. "We must make full advantage of the fog which is smothering the streets above us."

Bedlam nudged Mickelwhite in the ribs, a hungry look in his eyes.

"Loyal Legionnaires, you have all been blessed with qualities that are rejected in the world above our heads. So-called 'polite society' has no place for you if you can pick a pocket, or open a safe, or use your physical strength to make others empty their overstuffed pockets… Talents that we welcome here in the Under!" The crowd erupted again.

Mickelwhite glanced around him at the inhabitants of the Under – cutpurses and cut-throats; men and women from all walks of life who'd found they were no longer welcome in the city. And the street kids, hundreds of them, like John Bedlam and the others in Mickelwhite's small brigade – Ruby Johnson, the thief; Jimmy Dips, the scavenger; Hans Schulman, the German immigrant; Munro, the hunchback. Outcasts, runaways and throwaways.

Yes, thought Mickelwhite bitterly, London had treated them all badly in the past.

"Today," Sweet continued, "is the day when you can get your own back. Is there some trinket in the shop window that you have always desired? Take it. It's yours! Is there someone on the surface who has treated you badly? Find them. Repay them!"

Mickelwhite could not distinguish his own voice from the swell of raw emotion that surrounded and engulfed him, filling the vast cavernous space of the sanctuary.

Then, in his deep tenor voice, Mr. Sweet began to quote the Legion Code: the rules that were burned as deeply into their minds as the brand on their palms.

"No weakness in our hearts!

No mercy for our enemies!

No law to bind us!

No prison to hold us!

No grievance to go unavenged!

No Watcher to be left alive!"

Then he continued: "And when London is on its knees and begging for mercy, then we will show them the true power of the Legion…"

Mickelwhite didn't hear the rest of the rousing speech. Only a few of Mr. Sweet's promises permeated the roar of his own thoughts. Reign of fear… Death… Victory… The Feast of Ravens…

In contrast, the personal promise running through Mickelwhite's mind was clear and razor-sharp. *I'll find you, Ben Kingdom.*

The dawn came early. A white dawn, drowning in fog.

It had been an uncomfortable night and Ben stretched as he emerged from his tent, trying to roll some of the stiffness from his body. He had hardly slept. It was impossible to rest when the city beneath him was groaning in pain.

The disturbances had begun a few hours after the fog had started to rise. It was sporadic at first; a shout here, a cry there. Mothers looking for missing children, husbands searching for wives, all lost and confused in the mists. The city was bewildered, scared, staggering blind, falling over itself in the gloom. Then came the sounds of crime, as pickpockets and burglars took advantage of the confusion.

Jonas had staggered home some time in the small hours, drained and alone. Ben had welcomed him with relief – but there was still no news of Nathaniel.

So Ben had continued to count every long hour, hoping that his brother would return. They had slept side by side nearly every day of their lives and Ben could never really settle until Nathaniel was beside him, snoring and farting.

But morning had come and Nathaniel was still out there. Somewhere.

Ben saw that Jago Moon was already up and about. The old man was stripped to the waist, his broad shoulders and barrel chest apparently oblivious to the cold. As Ben watched, Moon dunked his whole head into a bucket of freezing water, then shook himself dry. Still dripping, Moon settled on a low stool and drew out a disreputable-looking knife, which he began to slowly scrape over his scalp, leaving his head as stubbly as his chin.

Hearing Ben's approach, Moon gave him a grin as he tugged on his shirt. "Grab a seat, son, I've got some porridge on the go." He passed Ben a tin plate and a spoon. "I reckon we're going to need a good start today."

Ben ate with the enthusiasm and elegance of a stray dog. He was licking up the last morsels when Molly ran over.

"Mother Shepherd wants both of you," she said. "She's waiting for you there." Molly pointed to the spire of St Bride's church, rising up out of the clouds of fog like a tower of hatboxes stacked on top of each other.

"Any word on Nathaniel?" Ben asked.

"I don't know," said Molly. "Mother Shepherd just said that she needs to see you *now*."

With a sense of urgency Ben and Jago Moon sprinted across the rooftops, using the ladders and planks that the Watchers had secreted all over the city heights. Ben had a cold hard feeling in his stomach. Then he heard Josiah and he braced himself for the worst.

The mighty angel who lived alongside them had earned the name the Weeping Man for good reason; he wept over the things that wounded the heart of his God, the Uncreated One. Josiah was crying now, a harrowing lament for a city being swallowed by evil.

As they reached the church tower, they saw that Mother Shepherd and the Weeping Man were waiting patiently for them. So too were Lucy Lambert, Ghost and a dozen or so other Watchers who Ben recognized as leaders of the other eyries scattered across London.

"We don't know where this monstrous fog has come from, but we can be certain that the Legion are at work," Mother Shepherd announced. "A report has come in from our spy that Legionnaires are using the fog like a cloak while they terrorize London street by street, doing their utmost to drive the city into a state of pandemonium."

"And with their network of tunnels, the Legion is free to strike and then slink back into their holes like the rats they are," Moon growled.

"Send word to every Watcher in London," said Mother

Shepherd, a steel edge to her voice. "The people of London are in distress like never before; it is up to *us* to help them in any way that we can. We have to go down into that foul fog and bring as many as we can up onto the safety of the roofs. And if the Legion try to stop us…then we will resist them. By whatever means necessary."

"We could use the Liberator," said Ben. "We could use a dozen Liberators!"

"And if we had them, we would," Mother Shepherd agreed, "but we didn't know that it would be needed so soon. It just isn't ready…" There was a moment's silence and Ben wondered quite how costly the delay might prove to be.

"However," Mother Shepherd went on, "your father and his team of engineers have been working flat out since dawn and we have scavengers searching for the remaining materials he needs."

Ben smiled. That was typical of his pa. But his smile soon dropped away as worry for his brother resurfaced. From across the city, screams and cries echoed. A thousand tongues calling out in fear. Breaking glass. Shrill police whistles. Running battles. Sounds of violence and conflict.

And somewhere in all that danger was Nathaniel. His father had a role which only he could fulfil, leading the

Watcher engineers as they worked on the Liberator – it was up to Ben, then, to find his brother and bring him home.

"Nathaniel…" The word escaped Ben's lips, and Mother Shepherd took a step closer, reaching out to place her hand on his shoulder.

"Ben," she said, with a note of caution.

"I know," said Ben, "I'm not ready, but I have to find my brother—"

Mother Shepherd stopped him. "None of us is ever truly prepared for what our futures hold, Benjamin, but ready or not, this is your time to act. Go. Help anyone you can. And find Nathaniel."

In spite of everything, Ben felt a sudden surge of joy. Action at last!

And, he thought, flexing the fingers of his right hand, a chance to see if his victory at Tower Bridge had been a fluke.

"Let's get to work," he said.

Silently, the small party of Legionnaires surfaced from a manhole cover; just one of a thousand secret entrances into the world of the Under. Careful so as not to let the heavy metal scrape and give the game away, they climbed out into the street. Mickelwhite and Bedlam were followed by the rest of their brigade: Jimmy Dips, his weasel face testing the air, and the broad-shouldered Hans Schulman. Bringing up the rear was Ruby, moving with feline stealth.

They emerged from their black tunnel into a landscape painted white.

"Blimey," said Bedlam, "Mr. Sweet wasn't joking when he said it would be foggy out."

"Keep your voice down," hissed Mickelwhite.

"Why?" said Ruby Johnson. "I can barely see you and I'm standing next to you."

"She's got a point, Captain," sniffed Jimmy Dips, but all his comment earned him was a swift backhand from Mickelwhite.

"If I want your opinion I will ask for it," he snorted. Although he had to admit that Jimmy was right.

For a moment they stood there, bewildered by the fog-entombed world. The clouds flowed around their feet as they moved. Mickelwhite had the sensation that he was in the clutches of a living wetness that licked and probed at his skin. The air was sticky with coal dust and the poisonous fumes of industry. It reeked of fish and the privy.

As they listened to London staggering blindly around them, Mickelwhite began to smile; a spiteful slash of pink in his marble white face. He could hear the sounds of terror.

"Is that you, Charlie?" called a woman's voice. "I can't see you, love. Who's there?"

"Where am I?" said an elderly man. "Is this Houndsditch? Can anyone help me get to Houndsditch?"

"Billy!" Another female voice, higher this time and edging towards hysteria. "Where are you, Billy? I told you not to wander off."

Then came a symphony of breaking glass.

"Oi! Mind out! What do you think you're playing at?"

A scuffle. The sounds of fists and feet.

"Come back here!"

"It's time to follow orders," hissed Mickelwhite.

With that, the boys checked their knuckledusters and drew leather coshes from their belts.

"What are you waiting for, Miss Johnson?" said Mickelwhite.

"I'm a thief," Ruby replied. "Let me do what I do best." And without waiting for permission, she padded away.

"Leave her," said Mickelwhite. "This is a job for the boys anyway. Remember our mission, gentlemen. Let panic rule and the Watchers fall!"

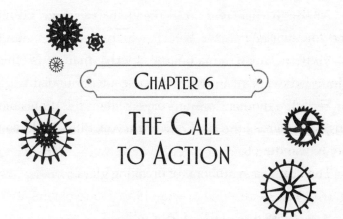

CHAPTER 6

THE CALL TO ACTION

Ben could feel the excitement coursing through his veins as he dropped a rope ladder over the side of the building and watched it disappear into the mist. This was his chance to put some of his training into practice, *at last*. Of course, he thought with a grin as Lucy Lambert joined him, good company never went amiss either.

Lucy tucked her crossbow-pistol snugly into its shoulder holster and made a quick count of the weighted bolts strapped round her waist. "Ready?" she said.

Ben tapped the expandable quarterstaff clipped to his own belt. "Always," he replied, and together they began to climb down into the gloom.

Although there wasn't a breath of wind to stir it, the fog swirled around Ben. It was probably his mind playing tricks on him, but he sensed that there was ghostly movement in the mist itself – figures that were present one moment only to vanish the next. With each step downwards the fog grew thicker and Ben could feel his exhilaration being leached away. It was as if dread had seeped into the very bones of the city, carried by the strange fog.

Perhaps that was why he could hear sounds of panic from every direction.

A child crying for its mother. A shout from a bedroom window, the words a tangled mess of terror and confusion. A window breaking. Noises of violence and fear.

When they were both on the ground, Ben and Lucy exchanged a glance and Ben saw his own feelings mirrored on Lucy's soft face. "Stick close," he said. "I'll look after you."

Lucy smiled and lowered her goggles. "There's a first time for everything."

Jago Moon clambered down the ladder behind them, his cane held at the ready. Ben knew the sword that it hid and the skill with which Moon could wield it.

Through the shifting mist, Ben quickly saw the source of the latest sound of broken glass – the shopfront opposite had just been smashed. It was a pawnbroker's, one of a hundred such establishments where the poor exchanged their meagre valuables for less than half their worth, along with the empty hope that they might one day be reunited with them. They all heard the sounds of a scuffle from within and the three Watchers turned as one, pulling up their scarves to cover their faces.

It wasn't possible, Ben knew, but it felt as if the vapour was trying to stop him, clawing at his jacket and tangling his legs with every step. Just for a second, out of the corner of his eye, Ben thought he spotted a figure, standing motionless and watching him struggle through the mist. It looked as if they were wearing a velvet jacket and had the most incredible emerald eyes. Then he blinked and they were gone.

In spite of the phantoms, and the clinging fog, Ben was determined to reach the shop. He ploughed forwards, grabbed the handle and flung the door open. In here the mist was thinner. Like most pawnshops, it was crammed to the rafters with a random assortment of forlorn treasures. Shelves heaved with the sheer weight of ornaments, candlesticks, crockery and knick-knacks. There were fur coats and hats on stands and hangers; a glass-topped counter beneath which lay watches and rings and hatpins and long-lost silver spoons; and it was all presided over by a rather moth-eaten stuffed bear, standing silently in the corner.

The shopkeeper was a short man with the most enormous pair of mutton chop whiskers. He was certainly no match for the bullies who had him backed up against the wall. There were four of them – all much bigger and older than Ben.

In the past Ben had always relied on his mouth to talk his way out of trouble – or more often *into* trouble, if he was honest. However, now that he was a Watcher, Ben had a few more tricks up his sleeve. He extended his quarterstaff with a flicking motion. It was a tasty weapon if you knew how to use it, and thanks to Jago Moon, Ben did.

"Come on then!" Ben yelled and charged straight for the bullies. He span his quarterstaff round his head and managed to bring a hatstand crashing to the floor. One of the robbers turned and laughed. Ben didn't recognize his face, but the black cowl he wore was enough to identify him as one of the Legion.

Ben tried a swift jabbing motion with his staff, and caught the Legionnaire in the stomach, winding him… and enraging him. With a roar, the Legionnaire leaped on Ben, swinging at him with a leather cosh. Ben blocked the first blow, ducked the second, and caught the third square on the jaw. His head spun and he thought that he might actually black out. He looked behind him for Lucy and Moon, expecting them to be striding into the fray, but he could hear the sounds of fighting outside the shop now and knew that help wasn't coming yet.

Ben raised his quarterstaff again even as his legs gave way beneath him and he collapsed to the ground. With a snort of contempt, the Legionnaire left him there and returned his attentions to the pawnbroker, who was still being menaced by the other three looters.

As Ben watched the Legionnaire walk away, he flexed the fingers of his right hand and felt a telltale pins-and-needles throbbing. This was how it always started: a stabbing sensation which intensified until Ben was no longer able to contain it. It was the reason why the Watchers were convinced he was their long-awaited leader, the one who would "bring the Legion tumbling down", to quote the prophecy.

Right, thought Ben, his head still woozy. *Here's someone who deserves a tumble.*

He closed his eyes and raised his right hand, rolling his fingers into a tight fist. Ben could feel the pressure growing inside him, feel the furious crackling of supernatural electricity as it filled his right hand with strength that was not his own.

He *needed* this to work. Not just for the sake of poor old

mutton chops, but for himself. For the Watchers. Ben had to know that the battle of Tower Bridge had not been a coincidence.

Inside the shop the pawnbroker's cries of anguish were growing louder. Outside the shop the fighting was getting worse…

Just as Moon had taught him, Ben listened, he stayed focused…

Now! Ben willed the full force of the Uncreated One to be unleashed.

He opened one eye a slit, just to see if there had been any effect and saw…the pawnbroker slumped on the floor while the ruffians helped themselves, tipping trays of medals and jewellery into hessian sacks. At that instant the remainder of the front window exploded inwards and Ben felt a shower of broken glass raining down upon him. More Legion hands reached in through the jagged hole and snatched what they could. Ben could hear coarse laughter followed by running feet. What he could not hear was Moon or Lucy.

Ben struggled up onto his knees and raised his right hand again, aiming it at the thug who had struck him down even though any sensation of power had long since passed. With a cruel sneer, the yob turned and raised his billystick again. "So you fancy seconds, do you?"

The blow never fell.

Jago Moon lashed out with his cane and intercepted the strike, stopping the cosh inches from Ben's head. Then, with lightning speed, Moon cracked his cane across the looter's wrist, making him drop the cosh with a yelp. For good measure, Moon delivered an uppercut to the lad's chin that clacked his teeth together.

"Best run home to your mother," Moon snarled.

"It's the mad blind one!" the Legionnaire declared as he realized who they were tangling with. He cradled his jaw, relieved that it wasn't dislocated, and began to make a break for the door at the back of the shop. Moon chuckled, delighted that his reputation went before him, as the looters stumbled over themselves to get away from his lashing cane. They got as far as the door and found their way blocked by a girl with an eyepatch, a quarterstaff and a look of grim determination.

"It's Scarface, too!" the Legionnaire declared as he recognized Lucy.

"Not your lucky day, is it?" she said.

Knowing when they'd met their match, the yobs grabbed their swag bags and escaped from the shop the only way that was left open to them – through the remains of the shattered front window.

Jago Moon went to the pawnbroker's side. "We're

friends," he said, helping the man back up onto his feet. Lucy tugged down her scarf and shook her long hair loose, extending her hand for Ben.

He refused it.

"Are you all right?" she asked.

"Fine," Ben snapped. "I don't need your help."

"That's not what it looked like," Lucy teased.

"I don't need anybody's help," said Ben and he stormed out into the road.

The Hand hadn't worked.

Where does that leave me? thought Ben. *Am I a failure or just a fake?*

He touched the Coin in his pocket, desperate for the comfort it gave him. A thrill of dark energy surged through his fingertips, and Ben relished the sense of power that came with it. The Coin made him feel strong again.

Ben licked his lips like a fox in a hen house.

Perhaps it wasn't a question of success or failure? Perhaps he was playing for the wrong side?

CHAPTER 7

DREAMS OF DESTRUCTION

The Under was empty. Almost.

Claw Carter swept through the tunnels, his long coat billowing behind him, driven hard by his furious rage.

Many in the Legion were afraid of him, Carter knew that. Afraid of his intelligence. Afraid of the dinosaur claw he wore where his hand used to be. Millions of years before, a *Megalosaurus* had used this claw to rip the life from its prey. Claw Carter used it for much the same purpose. But now he'd lost much of the respect, the fear, that he'd so carefully garnered. And it was all because of Mr. Sweet.

Mr. Sweet had made him a scapegoat for the Legion defeat at the battle of Tower Bridge. To add to that indignity, Sweet had also commandeered the Nightmare Child. Carter felt the swell of resentment inside his chest, as hot and heavy as a cannonball. Sweet could never have summoned that abominable creature without his knowledge of the Dark Library, the Legion's hidden vault of arcane and forbidden books.

Carter arrived at the rendezvous to find his fellow conspirator waiting for him. Obviously they had been waiting a while, Carter deduced from the slaughtered calf that was sprawled, half eaten, on the flagstone floor. Carter didn't give the unfortunate animal a second glance; he was no stranger to spilled blood.

Carter watched dispassionately as his partner in crime finished his meal of raw beef. Red and dripping from his feast, his hands were strangely proportioned, with fingers that were too long and too sharp. His feet, too, were elongated and narrow, hooked at the heel like some great bird's. His limbs were longer than those of a mortal man, the muscles thinner and more sinuous. Claw Carter had grown accustomed to this creature's company and almost took for granted the wings which emerged from his shoulders; battered and scarred as they were, the feathers not white, but grey.

However, even a man of Carter's experience, a man who had dined with the headhunters of New Guinea, couldn't help but be unnerved by his companion's face.

This was not an angel whose likeness would ever be found immortalized in stained glass. This was a fallen Seraphim, a being spoken of in whispers, having the form of a man but the head of a monstrous eagle. Grey Wing had once sung the praises of the Uncreated One, but now hated Him with such ferocity that it would rather dwell in the darkness and filth of the Under than ever have to beg forgiveness.

While Grey Wing continued to gnaw on a huge bone, his beak seeking out the juicy marrow inside, Claw Carter spoke. He behaved as if this were all perfectly natural, nothing more than two gentlemen engaged in a conversation over dinner, although no one outside of that room would have been able to recognize the words which he uttered. He was the only man who had ever mastered the language of the Feathered Men. There was no beauty to their tongue, it was as harsh and brutal as the Feathered Men themselves, and yet it had served Claw Carter well to learn it. When raising an army, a general had to be able to communicate with his troops.

"So," Carter began, Grey Wing observing him with one unblinking eye, "we failed in our last attempt to seize power." Grey Wing did not respond or appear to care. "Outwitted by a boy."

"The Kingdom child," Grey Wing said, pausing to spit out a lump of gristle. "He would make good eating."

"No!" Carter slammed his claw down on the table to emphasize his point. "Ben Kingdom could still be useful to us." As much as Ben had inconvenienced him, there was something about the lad which meant that Carter could never hate him. Ben Kingdom was an overcomer; he had a spirit that enabled him to rise above his circumstances, to keep fighting regardless of the odds. Carter felt a certain kinship with that.

"Ben Kingdom has…talents," Carter continued. "That much should be obvious even to you. Don't you remember how he defeated your Feathered Men at Tower Bridge? Surely you cannot forget how he used the Hand of Heaven and called down hailstones to drive you from the sky!"

Grey Wing remained silent, but paused to inspect a ragged hole in his wing, a souvenir of his last meeting with Ben Kingdom.

"I intend to harness that power for the Legion," Carter continued. "Just imagine what he could achieve as the Hand of Hell!"

"I thought that you had already tried that…and failed."

It was a stinging remark but Carter let it pass. He

hadn't realized what Ben meant to him before; he had seen the boy merely as a means to an end. Carter felt differently now…

"You and I both know that it is never too late for someone to walk the Legion path," said Carter. "We have a defrocked bishop in our number, as well as the burglars and thieves. Ben will come round to our way of thinking, just you wait and see."

Grey Wing cocked his head and fixed Carter in his gaze.

"But time is running out for you, isn't it, human? That is why you have come crawling to me again."

Carter couldn't deny it. After years of inaction, Mr. Sweet had suddenly made his move. "I underestimated Sweet, I have to confess. I don't think any of us expected him to remove the other members of the Council so… decisively."

"Really?" Grey Wing scoffed. "You imagine that you are the only man in the Legion to have dreams of power? There's hardly a soul in the Under who doesn't conspire against someone!"

"Sweet and I are *not* the same," Carter said emphatically.

Grey Wing busied himself with a bone.

"Sweet wants the Crown of Corruption so that he can make himself a king. He wants to take one monarch and merely replace them with another… He thinks small. My plan is somewhat…different. It is a plan that I am certain you will be able to align yourself with, you and all your feathered brothers."

Grey Wing did not look up from his feasting.

"I want nothing less than Hell on earth."

Grey Wing stopped mid chew. "Tell me more."

"Mr. Sweet will use the Legion and the Feathered Men to establish an empire for himself. But I want chaos. I want ruin." Carter showed his passion in every word. "I want destruction."

"I like it!" said Grey Wing, his cold eyes suddenly ablaze. "The best way to wound the Uncreated One would be to lay His creation to waste!"

"I knew you would appreciate the simplicity of my goal."

"But why would you choose such a path?"

"My reasons are my own," said Carter. "Suffice it to say that I have a score to settle."

"The thirst for revenge," said Grey Wing with approval, "one of the few emotions that I'm still able to feel." Tossing aside the remains of his meal, the ancient Feathered Man gave Carter his full attention. "So," he said, "you plan to remove Mr. Sweet?"

"Permanently."

"I have just one demand then, if you want my support," said Grey Wing. "After you kill Sweet, can I eat him?"

"Which would you prefer," asked Claw Carter. "Leg or breast?"

CHAPTER 8

LOST IN
THE MADNESS

The Nightmare Child skipped on. This fog was such fun. He had spent five delicious minutes playing peek-a-boo with an old man in his nightshirt. While the man was washing his face, the Nightmare Child had stood behind him, making sure that the man caught a fleeting glimpse of him in the mirror each time he rubbed his bleary eyes. The old man thought he was going insane.

The old man was right.

After that he sat in a nursery and helped the china dolls to walk on their own. They went looking for the nanny and she squealed when they found her.

Then he fancied a change of scenery and set out to find

the lowest drinking house imaginable. The Blue Dog was full of the most desperate drinkers. All he had to do was whisper in one man's ear, then sit back in the corner to watch the fun. The fight that ensued left no one standing and reduced the furniture to matchwood.

The Nightmare Child clapped his tiny hands together. "More!" he said. "I want more."

"Any sign of Nathaniel?" The words came tripping over Ben's lips in their haste to be spoken.

Jonas Kingdom shook his head sadly. "No one's heard from him, none of the scouting parties have seen him."

Ben stood by his father's side on the roof of Peek, Frean & Co's, the biscuit manufacturers. The warmth of the factory beneath their feet and the sweet aroma of baking surrounded them, binding them together in a brief moment of calm. It had been a long hard day and it showed no sign of letting up. Jonas looked besieged, as if he was aching inside and out.

Ben had followed in the footsteps of Lucy and Mr. Moon from morning till evening, feeling like a failure. True, they had rescued nearly a dozen people and helped a dozen more. True, they had even caught a few Legionnaires and sent them packing. But Ben found it hard to move beyond that moment when his special power – the Hand that the Watchers were all counting on him to use – had failed to work again. And everywhere they went it was the same story – no sign of Nathaniel.

When they had wearily climbed back onto the rooftops to grab something to eat, Ben's heart had leaped to see that his father was there before him. And then fallen just as quickly when he saw that Nathaniel wasn't with him.

"We'll find him, Pa," Ben promised now.

Jonas ruffled Ben's hair and drew his son close. "You're all I've got," he said. "You and your brother." Then he dug into his bag and pulled out a hunk of bread and a slab of cheese.

They lapsed into silence again as they ate. The landscape below them was bizarre, the streets and low roofs entirely submerged in swirling limbs of fog. Ben ran his hand through his red-gold hair and longed for his old billycock hat.

"He'll be alright," he said, as much to reassure himself as his pa. "Nathaniel can handle himself."

"I know, but I won't get any rest until I see him again," said Jonas.

The fog had continued to suffocate the city all day. Londoners, being Londoners, had been doing their best to keep life going as normal, but it was getting harder by the hour. It was more than just the blindness and the disorientation, more than the thieves and the looters who had chosen to make the most of this dark opportunity. Fear was rising too; Ben could almost smell it over the stink of the Thames. Creeping up through the floorboards of every house, oozing through the alleyways, seeping into the foundations of the great city...

A stone rattled somewhere on the roof behind them and Ben spun, his hand reaching for his quarterstaff. In the dim evening light, he could make out a silhouette, standing silently. "Who's there?" Ben challenged.

The figure moved closer, and Ben left his weapon on his belt.

Lucy smiled. "I'm sorry, I didn't mean to disturb you. I thought I was alone up here."

"Don't worry," said Jonas. "Any news of my boy?"

It was Lucy's turn to shake her head.

"What're you up to then?" asked Ben. "It's not like you to be skiving off." It sounded like more of a challenge than Ben had meant it to.

"I do have a life too, you know," Lucy responded curtly. But then she softened. "This is my favourite roof – I just like to come here by myself sometimes."

"To spy on the Legion?"

Lucy shook her head. "To smell the biscuits."

"I could murder a garibaldi," said Ben. He felt bad about being rude to Lucy. He wished he hadn't taken his frustration out on her and he gave her a smile by way of an apology. "Friends?" he said.

Lucy nodded and gave him a smile of her own.

A scream rose up from the streets and their smiles vanished.

"We have to find Nathaniel before night falls," said Ben.

CHAPTER 9

HIDE-AND-SEEK

"So you think that Nathaniel might have come here?" Ben asked his father.

"I'm not sure, Ben," Jonas replied, "but he was scavenging for rope and this is a good place to get it, so..."

"So we've nothing to lose by looking," said Lucy, as she pulled out the tight bundle of her escape ladder and got busy securing it.

Ben knew the maritime chandlery down by the docks – everyone did. If he'd been sent out to find some rope, he certainly would have thought of here. Hopefully Nathaniel had too.

Lucy double-checked her knots and then let the ladder clatter to the ground, where it was lost in the fog.

"After you, m'lady," said Ben with a bow.

"Oh no, after you." Lucy played along.

"For goodness' sake, pack it in, you two," said Jonas Kingdom, swinging his big frame over the edge of the chandlery roof and onto the ladder. "There's work to be done."

"You always get me into trouble, Ben Kingdom," said Lucy quietly as she followed Ben down the rungs.

"An' that's why you like me," said Ben. "You good girls always go for the bad lads."

"You wish."

The lightness of Ben's words did nothing to disguise the knot of worry in his gut. And when they reached the cobblestones, they both fell silent.

Ben felt overwhelmed. Once more, he was only a few feet away from people shouting, weeping, fighting, and yet he couldn't see any of them. He had already spent countless hours searching for Nathaniel in this cursed fog. How was he ever going to find him?

The day was failing fast and the opal glow of the gas lamps only added to the confusion, creating globes of flickering light which merely deepened the shadows all around. At his side, Lucy took on a ghostly form as the fog came between them. Simultaneously they reached for each other's hand.

One voice rose above the others in the chaos. Somewhere a small child, no more than two years old, Ben guessed, was crying for her mother, a terrible forlorn wailing. They were here for Nathaniel, Ben knew, but they were still Watchers.

"Stay still," Jonas shouted to the petrified child. "Let me come to you," and he set off in the direction of the cries.

"Wait," said Ben, holding him back. He took a coil of thin rope from his pack. "Tie this to your belt, Pa. You too, Lucy. If we get separated in this we'll never find each other again."

Jonas quickly secured the line before disappearing into the fog, Lucy releasing the rope hand over hand behind him. Then they heard the child's cries again, but this time it seemed to Ben that they were coming from the opposite direction. The fog was playing cruel tricks, he realized. There was only one thing for it.

"Stay here," he told Lucy. "We stand a better chance of finding that poor kid if I check the other way, but I need you to keep guard at the foot of the ladder. It's our only way out of here." The mist swirled between them, as if to emphasize his point. He took out another coil of rope, tied one end to his belt and passed the other end to Lucy, before he plunged into the sea of chaos.

"Hold on," Ben called to the lost child. "I'm coming to help you!"

He pushed forwards, and this time he had no doubt – the fog *was* working against him. Snake-like tentacles entwined themselves around his arms and legs, making Ben fight for every step. Then, just as suddenly, the grip was released and Ben stumbled forwards.

Behind him he heard Lucy calling him, desperation in her voice.

"Ben!" she shouted. "The line has gone slack. Where are you?"

Ben looked at his waist and saw that the rope was gone. The spectral fingers of the fog must have loosened the knots.

At that moment, a sailor, who had decided to solve the problem of being lost by drinking himself stupid, staggered into Ben, spinning him round by the shoulder. The sailor belched an apology of sorts but left Ben dizzy and disorientated. And lost.

"Pa!" he shouted. "Lucy!"

Two voices replied "Ben!" but Ben didn't have time to regain his bearings. From somewhere far too close, he heard a horse whinny in distress and the frantic voice of its master trying to calm it. The sound of hoofs drumming on the cobbles echoed through the fog, followed by a terrible crash as a carriage overturned creating huge billows and swirls in the mist around Ben. The fog cleared just enough for Ben to make out passengers and the fallen animal as they cried out in pain. For a fleeting instant Ben thought he saw a face from his past, a face with chestnut hair and emerald eyes looking straight at him. Ben blinked, and it was gone. Another ghost in the fog.

Then came the laughter. Not the sweet melody of Lucy Lambert, but a cruel and ugly sound which chilled Ben to his core.

Ben thought he saw a figure flash past him.

"Lucy?" Ben called out. "Nathaniel, is that you?"

The figure passed closer. Not Lucy or Nathaniel, Ben realized, but a peculiar child with curly blond hair. And yet it couldn't be the same little kid who'd been lost and wailing, could it? Ben's blood ran cold as he caught a glimpse of the tiny figure, skipping through the mist. "Are you playing hide-and-seek?" the strange child trilled.

"Who are you?" Ben challenged, his voice almost cracking with fear.

"You'll have to keep seeking if you want to find your brother, Ben Kingdom," the child taunted. "I haven't finished playing with Nathaniel yet."

Ben's heart turned to ice.

The child laughed again and Ben spun round, desperate to catch up with him, in spite of the dread that was squirming in his mind like worms in old cheese.

The laughter came from everywhere and nowhere as Ben blundered through the fog in pursuit. He knew that he was moving further away from Lucy and his pa, but here was a chance to find Nathaniel. He might not get another.

Twice Ben collided with other bodies, as disorientated and distressed as he was. Twice he picked himself up and stumbled on. It was only one thought that gave him the strength to carry on: *Follow the creature, rescue Nathaniel.*

Nathaniel in chains. In the dark... Alone... Except for the rats... And that evil child...who certainly wasn't flesh and blood... What might such a creature be capable of? And what had it done with his brother?

It was such an all-consuming thought that Ben didn't realize that while he was following the fiendish child someone else was stalking him. He didn't see the hand that snatched the Watcher satchel from his shoulder. And he didn't see the club rise and fall, or hear the footsteps running away.

But he felt the blow, and watched in confusion as his world turned from white to black as he fell unconscious and the floor rushed up to welcome him.

CHAPTER 10

THE MIDNIGHT VISITOR

The Prime Minister, Lord Robert Gascoyne-Cecil, was pacing anxiously in his private rooms at the Savoy Hotel. He could still hear the baying voices that had been raised at him in the Houses of Parliament that day, the jeering boos and ballyhoos. Disorder was spilling through the London streets and the police were losing control. Everyone expected *him* to resolve the situation, but, in truth, he had no idea how to restore calm or stem the rising violence. Only one man seemed to have a plan for this dark time, and the Prime Minister was waiting for him now.

The knock came an hour later than they had agreed, but even so the Prime Minister was relieved to hear it, rushing to answer the door himself. "Thank you for seeing me at this late hour," he said, ushering in his special advisor.

"The pleasure is all mine," Mr. Sweet replied.

"Please allow Jackson to take your coat and hat," said Lord Cecil. "Will you join me in having a brandy, to fight this inclement weather?"

The stony-faced butler silently took Sweet's fur-collared greatcoat and silk top hat. A maid appeared with a glass of golden liquid on a silver tray. Sweet swirled the brandy in the glass and inhaled deeply.

Cecil led him through to an oak-panelled study. A fire burned brightly in the grate. A black slate clock sombrely ticked off the minutes. Mr. Sweet made himself comfortable in a wing-backed leather chair. He drank deeply and then waved his glass for more.

The Prime Minister took up the chair opposite, suddenly feeling like he was the visitor. The maid refilled Sweet's glass.

"Leave the decanter," said Sweet.

The maid looked to the Prime Minister for permission, her eyes as wide as a frightened deer's. Lord Cecil nodded.

"So, Mr. Sweet," Cecil began.

"So?"

"Please tell me this plan of yours. The police force is in tatters, looting is rife, there's even talk of some sort of plague of lunacy…a brain fever that is leaving men insensible. To be honest, I'm at a complete loss."

"I know you are," Sweet replied, settling back with his brandy.

The Prime Minister waited.

Mr. Sweet smiled.

"Now, look here," Lord Cecil began. "I am grateful for your help, but I am not in the habit of being toyed with, I—"

A strange knocking interrupted him.

"What the…? What is that?"

"I hope you don't mind," said Mr. Sweet, rising to his feet, his bull-like presence cowing the Prime Minister in his chair. "But I took the liberty of inviting a guest."

"What are you babbling on about, man? A guest?"

"An expert on disasters of this sort," Sweet continued, walking over to the window. "I'm certain that you'll be enthralled by what he has to say."

"Where the deuce is that knocking coming from?" said Lord Cecil.

"From the window, Prime Minister," said Sweet, towards the glass; yet beyond there seemed to be nothing but the blackness of the night and the impenetrable wall of fog.

"But we are on the third floor! What is this madness?" Cecil demanded, going over to the window to see for himself.

"How clever of you to guess," said Sweet cryptically.

The Prime Minister peered out into the darkness and then recoiled in shock, unable to comprehend what he was seeing.

There was a figure on the other side of the glass. A boy of perhaps five or six years old. A boy with wings.

Lord Cecil staggered back in disbelief, all colour draining from his cheeks.

Silently the boy lifted his hand and tapped again upon the glass. His face was rounded with the fat of youth, but his blue-black eyes were old and brimming with savage intelligence. The eyes of something monstrously evil, Cecil thought.

"We mustn't keep our visitor waiting," said Sweet as he threw the window up with a theatrical flourish. A wave of fog poured over the sill and began to spill across the carpet.

The Prime Minister backed away towards the fireplace. Desperately he grabbed a poker and brandished it in front of him.

"Help!" he shouted. "Help me!"

"It's rather too late for that," said Mr. Sweet. "Please allow me to introduce you to the Nightmare Child."

On cue, the peculiar boy flew into the room and landed silently.

Cecil wanted to slash out at the creature with the poker, to stove its small head in and then run for his life, but he found that fear rooted him to the spot. Useless, the poker dropped from his hand. All that the Prime Minister could do was stare.

The Nightmare Child was small and plump. Beautiful blond curls covered his head. He was dressed, of all things, in a sailor suit, as though some proud mother had prepared him for a photographer. But the Prime Minister instinctively knew that this creature had no mother; it had been spawned. To Lord Cecil's horror, the small boy smiled at him.

"Come and play with me," said the Nightmare Child.

"Dear God, help me," Cecil whispered.

CHAPTER 11

THE LIVING FOG

Ben wasn't sure how long he had been unconscious but he knew that his head was hammering. He struggled to sit upright, and found that the fog was holding him down, wrapping him in its folds like an Egyptian mummy. All around him, the chaotic screams and shouts had subsided, only to be replaced by a groaning that was somehow worse. The moaning of lost souls and the shuffling of their feet in the gloom.

Gritting his teeth, Ben wrenched himself free of the fog's grip. Clambering to his feet, he found a wall to guide him and blundered along it. Fingers of mist tugged at him as he fled, pulling at his coat, his face, his hair, until Ben was wet with fearful sweat. After an agonizing minute that felt like a year, Ben found a door. To his relief, it swung open at his push and he almost fell inside, shutting the door firmly behind him.

The tailor's shop that he was standing in had fallen prey to looters, most of its rolls of fabric long gone, the till empty, the furniture overturned. Ben wasted no time in dragging a broken table over to the door to wedge it shut and slamming closed the wooden shutters over the broken window, blocking out the dim glow of the street lamps.

He had lost most of his Watcher kit when his bag had been stolen, but Ben still had a stump of candle in his pocket and a lucifer to light it with. The match flared as the wick began to burn and Ben slumped down, feeling safe at last as he admired his makeshift barricade.

As if in response, the fog began to force its way under the front door. Tendrils of mist, like blind maggots, eased themselves through the gap between wood and stone. As Ben watched, more of those cold wet fingers began to tease themselves around the window shutters. Another long digit pushed itself through the keyhole.

Looking around, Ben considered his options. He thought for a moment about ripping up some of the remaining tailor's cloth to plug the gaps, but he knew instinctively that it wouldn't be enough. There was no way that he would be able to stop the room from filling with the living fog.

You can keep this for a lark, Ben thought and headed quickly for the stairs. He needed to get up onto the roof and fast.

It was a narrow four-storey building and Ben took the stairs three at a time. The attic room, when he arrived, was damp and cold, but still nicer than any room Ben had ever lived in, he noticed wistfully. Like most top-floor bedrooms, half of the ceiling sloped down, following the line of the roof, and a small window jutted out at right angles. On the other side of the glass there was nothing but white.

"Here we go again," said Ben as he pushed the window open. The fog tumbled in and Ben scrambled out.

The window ledge was slick with the oily residue of the mist and his feet struggled to find a hold in spite of his skyboots. Ben grasped the window frame and clung to it tightly. There was no sense of height in the sea of vapour, but Ben knew very well that one slip would still mean goodnight, Benjamin.

Having regained his balance, Ben began to haul himself up onto the roof. He put his hand on something wet and grimaced. He'd used to be a mudlark, shoving his hand into goodness knows what on a daily basis, but this still felt grim, as if the slates had been licked by some foul tongue.

Easy does it, he urged himself, as he repositioned his hand to get a better grip. Very carefully he started to shift his weight from his legs to his arms and ease himself higher. If he could make it as far as the chimney, hopefully he'd be above the fog and have something decent to hang on to while he tried to see if there were any other Watchers around to help him.

I've got the hang of this, thought Ben confidently. *Piece of—*

But he never got to finish that thought, because the finial he was levering himself up on cracked and came away in his hand. For a second, Ben's balance held, and then a tentacle of fog reached up and grabbed, yanking him backwards into the billowing white.

Ben had the sensation of being enveloped by clouds and he was struck by the thought that this might be what Heaven was like. Only in Heaven he supposed there was no chance of getting your brainpan smashed on the pavement – which was exactly what was about to happen to him.

As death opened wide its arms to greet him, Ben saw Nathaniel in his mind and heard the stomach-turning laughter of the child in the sailor suit.

This was not how it was meant to end.

Suddenly, the vapour around Ben stirred as a huge pair

of wings cut swathes through the air. Ben felt the rush of their downdraught and then sharp pain, his arms threatening to pop from their sockets, as Josiah yanked him upwards.

"That's two I owe you," said Ben with relief. "But how did you ever find me?"

"Have you never heard of guardian angels?" said Josiah as they finally broke free from the suffocating blanket of mist, leaving a mass of squirming white tendrils reaching for their ankles.

The Watcher spy was careful not to be seen. There were places in the Under that he could go without rousing any suspicions, but the cells were not one of them.

He had big feet and he planted them carefully. Caution was his only friend; he wouldn't have survived very long in the enemy camp without it. When the other Legion boys had gone above ground to play their part in the pandemonium, he had allowed himself to straggle at the back of the party. They would assume that he had got lost. They would not think that he had doubled back into the Under to see the prisoner.

There had been laughing and cheering in his barracks when Claw Carter told them who they had in chains.

Anything that hurt the Watchers was always greeted with delight, especially if it had the added bonus of bringing pain to Ben Kingdom.

The spy had met Ben. He liked Ben. Ben was the Hand of Heaven, he had no doubt about it. That was why the spy stayed in the Under regardless of the danger – because he believed in Ben. That was also why he was sneaking along the corridor with a stolen parcel of bread and cheese.

The Under was virtually deserted, although he knew that wouldn't be the case for long. Soon some of the Legionnaires would begin to return from their malicious labours. He hurried on.

He found the cell without too much difficulty. It was the one with the Feathered Man standing guard outside. The spy had anticipated this too and tossed it a bone, which it fell upon ravenously.

"Mr. Sweet sent me," he lied. "You understand?"

He had bought himself about sixty seconds, he guessed. While the creature was distracted, the spy approached the door and opened the slit which allowed prisoners to be observed. He spotted the poor lad, curled up in the corner on the straw.

"Quickly," the spy hissed, pushing his parcel through the gap, "I have brought food."

In a daze, the prisoner struggled onto his feet and stumbled over to the door. He picked up the cheese and held it before his face with an expression of sheer confusion, as if he had never seen this strange yellow substance before and had no idea what he should do with it.

"Eat," the spy mimed, holding his fingers to his mouth.

Tentatively the prisoner took a tiny nibble.

"Good," the spy encouraged. "Eat it all, yes. I will come back with some more when I can."

The spy knew his time was ticking away. He pushed his hand through the slit in the door and squeezed the prisoner's shoulder. "Stay strong, Nathaniel Kingdom, the Watchers will not leave you here. Have faith in your brother. *Trust Ben.*"

The Feathered Man finished his bone. The spy ran.

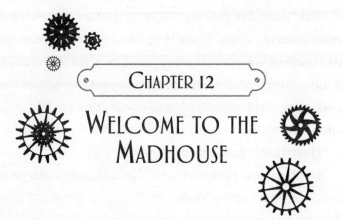

CHAPTER 12

WELCOME TO THE MADHOUSE

"Gentlemen, gentlemen." Mr. Sweet's deep tones rolled out across the chamber of the House of Commons. His words rested on top of the other voices and submerged them, like oil on water. "Gentlemen, calm please."

All eyes fell on him.

"What news do you have of the Prime Minister?" someone shouted from the backbenches.

"It is with regret that I must inform the House that Lord Cecil has suffered a most grievous bout of brain fever."

There were cries of alarm from all sides.

"But," said Mr. Sweet, raising his hand, "when I last spoke with the Prime Minister, even in his frail condition his concerns were all for this House and for the people of our great nation. He asked me if I would be his messenger and bring his plan to resolve this terrible crisis before you today."

"Hear, hear," came the cry.

"Furthermore, he asked me if I would do him the great favour of carrying the burden of office and stand as Prime Minister until he has recovered."

"And what did you say?"

"With a heavy heart," Mr. Sweet continued, "I felt that I had no choice but to consent to his wishes. Trusting, of course, that I have the support of this House."

An uncomfortable hush descended. Then one man rose to his feet and cleared his throat as if he was about to speak. Sweet locked him full in his gaze. There was a moment of unspoken warfare between the two men. One second later the minister dropped his head and sank back onto the bench.

The awkward silence stretched as Sweet scanned the chamber, looking for any other challengers who needed to be defeated. No eyes dared to meet his own.

"Aye," came a voice from the backbenches, quickly taken up across the House. "Aye!"

"And what of Lord Cecil now? Can you tell us any more about his condition?" asked one MP.

"Only that he needs rest and plenty of it," said Mr. Sweet. "Lord Cecil is even now receiving the most advanced treatment for his condition that medical science has to offer. Trust me," he said. "I've arranged it myself."

"Blimey," said the porter. "It's like Piccadilly Circus in here today."

"Tell me about it," said the driver of the cab. "I've got three more in the back, and there'll likely be a dozen more before the day is out if we keep going at this rate."

"It's this fog," said the porter, a strong man with arms like a bag of walnuts. "It's enough to send anyone potty, if you ask me."

"So who've you got in here, then?" asked the doctor, who'd come out to meet the cab. He was a young man who was earnestly growing a pointy beard in an attempt to be taken more seriously by his peers.

"Search me," said the driver, "I just pick 'em up. There's not one of them who knows who they are; they're all as nutty as a fruit cake. One of 'em swears he's the Prime Minister!"

They all laughed at that and the porter carefully drew

back the bolts on the cab door. "I'd stand back if I were you, doc," he warned. "You know they bite sometimes."

"I don't think I need to worry about that," said the doctor, although he did surreptitiously position himself so he was behind the porter. "As I have tried to explain before, these poor wretches are not animals to be put down, but are patients and must be treated appropriately. This isn't the Dark Ages, you know. I have in my possession Messrs Davis and Kidder's patent electric-medical machine." His voice grew more excited. "Imported from the United States of America, no less! I assure you that once they have experienced my reviving and refreshing application of electricity, these individuals will feel right as rain again."

"I'll take your word for it, doc," said the porter. "Come on then, Prime Minister," he said, taking Lord Cecil's limp hand. "Let's get you all tucked up. We've got a nice cell lined with cork and India rubber and it's got your name on it."

"Welcome to Bethlehem Lunatic Asylum," said the doctor, clasping the poor man's trembling hand and gazing into his blank, unfocused eyes. He shook his head sadly. "A terrible case of delusion. He doesn't look anything like Lord Cecil."

Mr. Sweet wasn't very impressed by democracy. You could never achieve something as audacious as stealing the entire British Empire if you started allowing other people to have a say in how things should be done. Luckily his fellow Members of Parliament were idiots to a man.

"What next, Mr. Prime Minister?" wailed a fat oaf on the Opposition bench. "How do you intend to resolve our current problem? The police are in turmoil; half of them are lost and most of the others are out of their minds."

"I have a simple plan which I *guarantee* will bring calm and restore order to the capital." Mr. Sweet paused to stroke his moustache. If there was to be any resistance to his schemes, this would be the trigger. "As of this moment I am declaring a state of martial law. I will put the army on the streets to bring peace by any means."

There was silence…followed by uproar.

"Bravo!" came the shouts. "Huzzah!"

"Thank you, gentlemen," said Sweet. "I knew that I could trust on common sense to prevail. Yes," he continued, "I shall deploy our soldiers – their presence alone will reassure the common Londoner. This very night I will give them their orders."

This too was greeted with much applause.

"Until the current spate of lawlessness has subsided,

I shall be declaring a curfew between the hours of nine at night and six in the morning. Any individual found on the streets between those hours will be presumed to be a looter or a housebreaker, and the police and the army will have the right to arrest such troublemakers. Curfew breakers are to be sentenced with the harshest measures available, and I will be recommending deportation to Australia for anyone found guilty." This too was received with many "hurrahs" from both sides of the House.

"Now, if you will excuse me, gentlemen, I must leave you. I have vital matters of state to attend to."

And with their cheers ringing in his ears, Mr. Sweet made his exit, his mind racing.

It was three days until the Feast of Ravens; the night when the forces of darkness would be at their strongest. The sacrifice was ready, and it was surely only a matter of time before it lured Ben Kingdom to him too.

Three days until Mr. Sweet took the Crown of Corruption for himself and claimed the awesome power of the Judas Coins as his own; the power to bend all men to his will, or so the Legion believed.

Three days until every head bowed to *him*.

Sweet strode through the corridors of the Palace of Westminster. He quickly arrived at the clock tower, known to the commoners as Big Ben – when every fool knew that was the name of the *bell* – and continued down into the basement. There Sweet opened the secret entrance to the Under, hidden behind false shelving, and descended the stone spiral staircase it revealed, taking a lantern from the wall to light his way.

For years, the Council of Seven had been in deadlock. *Do we dare use the Crown of Corruption? Who is capable of wielding such fearsome power?* Sweet gave a derisive laugh. With the Council dead and buried – after he'd taken the precaution of driving them mad and rendering them defenceless first – Mr. Sweet found that he was able to answer both of those questions instantly.

Yes!

I am!

The Legion had gathered the Coins from the furthest corners of the globe, where the Watchers had attempted to scatter them. Had they gone to such effort merely to lock them away behind another door, to leave them to rust? There was no point having a weapon, Sweet thought, if you weren't prepared to use it. One Coin was still missing, admittedly, but a tiger with one less tooth was *still* a tiger, and with everything else falling into place, he was not prepared to delay any more.

Eventually he arrived at a door, behind which lay the prize. Because not one member of the Council of Seven trusted any of the others, the door which kept the crown from the light of day was locked with seven locks and opened by seven keys. Mr. Sweet reached into his pocket and pulled out a jailer's ring, jangling with the full set. His former associates were no longer in a fit state to look after them.

Starting with the lock at the top, Mr. Sweet set to work.

The door itself was built from iron, solid and unyielding. Its only decoration was in the moulding of the seven keyholes, each one a representation of the seven glorious vices of the Legion. The first keyhole was in the shape of a bloated face with a distended, gorging mouth; it stood for gluttony. The next twisted face showed a pair of longing eyes; the symbol of envy. Pride came next, followed by sloth, lust and avarice. Finally he selected the key which he hadn't had to steal. This lock was forged in the shape of a face distorted with furious anger. That was his great gift to the Legion: wrath.

When the final bolt drew back, Mr. Sweet put his hand to the door and stepped inside. He lifted his lantern and let its light fall on the treasure.

In the middle of the chamber a simple stone plinth had been erected. On top of that sat a skull, and resting on that was the crown. It was a simple iron band, like the ancient crowns of old, and around its rim twenty-nine Roman coins had been set in place. Putting his lantern down, Sweet picked it up and examined it with reverence.

It was an evil thing, he recognized. He could feel the dark influence radiating from it and his own black heart rejoiced.

Claw Carter was so smug, thinking that *he* was the only one with any knowledge of the Legion lore. There was one prophecy which Sweet had very much taken to heart. He recited it out loud, the words echoing back to him.

"He who claims the crown on the raven night shall reign for ever more."

That will do for a start, Sweet thought.

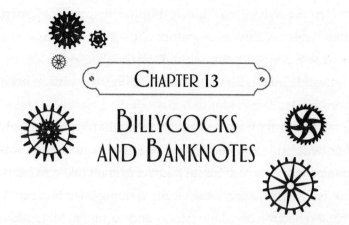

CHAPTER 13

BILLYCOCKS
AND BANKNOTES

The roof of Grosvenor House was alive with activity. Ben was with the others working flat out on the Liberator, using his knowledge as a barrel-maker to do his part. He looked up and saw his pa shouting orders left, right and centre, and his heart brimmed with pride. Ropes had been dropped down over the side of the mansion and Watchers were hauling up planks of wood, copper pipes, cables… Goodness only knew where they had managed to scrounge all of that. Everyone was focused on the task in hand; even little Molly Marbank was sitting with a group of girls getting busy with a needle and thread. She spotted him and held up her sewing for him to admire.

Ben waved to her. But despite being proud of what they were achieving together, he couldn't mask the sinking feeling that this was all too little too late.

He felt Lucy's hand on his shoulder then and he rose from his back-breaking labours. He had hardly stopped since Josiah had brought him back at the crack of dawn, and he ached from sawing and hammering. His head still throbbed from the blow that had knocked his lights out, but he wasn't about to start complaining. He felt guilty that he had caused Jago Moon and Josiah more trouble searching for him when there was so much to do here.

Ben had wanted to be out looking for his brother, but his work on the Liberator was vital. His skill as an apprentice cooper had come in useful and the quicker he got his part done, the quicker he could get back out and search again. In the meantime, it was Lucy who had been hunting for Nathaniel, with as many other Watchers as could be spared right across the city. All of them had been warned – *Beware the laughing child.*

Lucy looked as tired as he felt. It had been as long a day as Ben could remember and every Watcher cell was stretched to the limits. Every time Ben looked up he had seen more refugees being brought onto the roof for safety. And there would be more tomorrow, Ben had

Ben knew from her silence that Lucy's search had been fruitless.

"Sorry," she said quietly.

A sad sigh escaped Ben's lips before he could catch it.

"It must feel like you've got the weight of the world resting on you," said Lucy, "but we believe in you, Ben." She turned his face towards hers so she could look him directly in the eye. "And we *will* find Nathaniel, I promise."

Ben stretched his aching arms. "Don't you ever wish you had a normal life?" he asked. "Instead of this?"

"No," said Lucy without hesitation. "This is all I want – to stay here with—" She caught herself. "I mean, to stay here and help. I think, somehow, I was always meant to be a Watcher, if that makes sense."

It did. If Lucy had been the Hand of Heaven, Ben would have had no difficulty having faith in her. Although he wouldn't say it to her face, there was something about Lucy that Ben really admired. Life had thrown Lucy a few punches and she'd chosen not to take them lying down. She was a fighter, like he was. And she had hair the colour of honey.

"Right," said Lucy. "Close your eyes."

"Why?"

"Just do it for me," she said as she began to rummage

in the backpack where she kept her supplies. "Now hold out your hands."

Ben obeyed.

When he opened them he found himself holding an oddly-shaped package, wrapped in brown paper and string.

"Open it then," Lucy prompted.

Ben pulled at the string and drew back the wrapping. "Thank you, Lucy," he said softly as he looked at the contents. "I've never had one of these before."

"Yes, you have," she said. "You always wore your billycock when we first met."

"No," Ben explained. "I mean, I've never had a *present* before."

"Well, go on," Lucy urged. "Try it on."

The billycock was even more battered and worn than the one he had lost. Ben picked it up and put it on, feeling a sudden surge of delight, as if he had just been reunited with an old friend.

"I don't know what to say." He grinned.

"There's a first," said Lucy, smiling. "I'm glad you like it," she went on. "It belonged to my brother."

"I didn't know…"

"It's not something I talk about," said Lucy, "but I had a mother and father once, and a brother. You remind me of him sometimes."

"Because he was brave and strong?" suggested Ben.

"No," said Lucy, "because I always had to look out for him."

Ruby Johnson returned to the Under laden down with her takings. As always, Munro was waiting for her when she returned to the barracks. Ruby's squire struggled to his feet as she entered the room, hindered by his lame leg and his hunchback.

"Sit down, Miss Ruby," said Munro, hobbling to her side. "I've got the kettle on for you."

Ruby smiled thinly, but it was enough to light up the hunchback's face. For a few minutes no one said a word. Alexander Valentine lay asleep on his bunk, wheezing – his lungs were too weak for him to join the raids above. Buster, Munro's three-legged bulldog, was firmly ensconced in his favourite spot before the fire. Munro bustled around Ruby, cleaning a tin mug for her on the hem of his shirt and filling it with steaming tea. One of them was filling the air with the aroma of old cabbage, but it wasn't clear who the culprit was. Ruby had narrowed it down to two.

She took the cup gratefully. Munro looked on with big eyes, hungry for her attention. "You're good to me, Munro," Ruby said, and the crippled boy grinned proudly.

"Good day?" he asked, eyeing her bulging bag.

"The best," she replied, tipping out her stolen loot on the table between them. Together they counted her haul. One silver candlestick, three leather wallets, two gentlemen's watches, a dozen or so assorted hairpins, various brooches and a rather fine gent's silk scarf. Ruby picked the best of the wallets and gave it to Munro. Inside he found a crisp one-pound note.

"It's too much," gasped Munro.

"Nonsense," she replied, "not for all you do for me. Now do as you're told and put it in your stash." She stroked his cheek with a warm hand and Munro's skin flushed.

"Thank you, Miss Ruby," he said, and he shuffled over to the lockbox hidden under his pillow, where he kept all the tokens that she gave him.

Ruby sighed and divided up the rest of her ill-gotten gains. Half of what she stole went straight to the Legion funds; everyone in the Under was expected to pay their dues. One of the wallets she set aside for Mickelwhite; she had no time for him, but these acts of tribute kept the captain off her back. The gent's scarf she kept for herself – she had other plans for that.

Munro finished fiddling with his box and came to join her. "Did you see anyone today, Miss Ruby?" he asked.

Ruby threw back her head and laughed unconvincingly. It seemed such an innocent question but she knew what was behind it. "You can't see anyone up there," she said, "that's why the pickings are so easy."

Munro made a small noise at the back of his throat and then shuffled back to the fire. "Let me make you some soup," he said.

She had lied to Munro and she hated to deceive him, but what was she supposed to say? *Yes, I saw Ben Kingdom again today. I followed him. I wish I had spoken to him.*

The truth was that she had seen Ben every day since he'd left the Legion, but only ever from a distance. For reasons that she couldn't explain, she felt compelled to seek him out every time she went up onto the surface.

"I'm glad I've got you, Miss Ruby," said Munro, his twisted back to her while he chopped onions and fed them to the pot.

"And I'm glad I've got you," said Ruby, grateful that her friend couldn't see the faraway look in her eyes.

CHAPTER 14

THE HOUR OF NEED

Events were moving quickly and Claw Carter had no intention of being left behind. Fortunately, Mr. Sweet was so busy making his play for power that he wouldn't notice Carter's own manoeuvrings until it was far too late.

Mr. Sweet was so arrogant, assuming that he was the one with all the plans. Carter could out-think him and outwit him, he was certain of it. He ran his claw down his list of possible options.

Poison? Too unreliable.

Assassins? Too impersonal.

A knife? Too messy.

A deadly spider in his slippers? Too flamboyant.

The answer was simple. A single bullet to the head at long range.

Carter had already found the location for his shot. All he needed now was a way to lure Mr. Sweet out into the open. That was why he had decided to make a house call; the bargaining chip that he was after lay on the other side of a magnificent stained-glass door in Knightsbridge.

Carter hooked his claw into the bell pull and set the doorbell jangling. He waited for the sound of footsteps in the corridor beyond, or the silhouette of a butler through the glass. He wasn't surprised that no response came, however, with half of London in hiding. When the streets are running with rioters and lunatics, the last thing you do is answer the door, especially at this time of night. You never knew who might be calling…

Carter lifted his claw again and smashed it into the stained-glass window. A thousand shards of glass landed on the doormat as Carter sawed his way through the lead fretwork and ripped it from its frame. Then he reached through the gap and opened the lock.

Carter paused and read the single word on the mat beneath the glittering fragments: *welcome*.

Why, thank you, Mr. Sweet, thought Carter as he stepped over the threshold. *Thank you for leaving such a precious treasure unguarded.*

The corridor in front of him was long and dark in spite of the glow of the gas lamps. Carter stalked forward. He was never more alive than when he was on the hunt. For the joy of it, Carter dragged the tip of his claw along the oak-panelled wall, leaving a white scar in his wake.

Furtive noises led him to the drawing room. It was a grand chamber decorated in the very latest fashion. A huge green-leafed aspidistra sat in a stately pot on an occasional table, an ornate ormolu clock ticked sedately on the mantel above the fire, and a petrified footman was hidden rather inexpertly behind the curtains. Carter could see the tips of his polished shoes sticking out beneath the hem.

There could be no witnesses.

Carter was across the room in two bounds. A single horizontal slash cut the curtain in two above the spot where he estimated the man's head must be. The heavy material fell and Carter bundled the man to the ground, still wrapped in it. While the servant thrashed, Carter held the velvet fabric tight over the footman's nose and mouth. In less than a minute, according to the ormolu clock, the struggling stopped and the footman lay still.

Carter rose to his feet. Above his head a floorboard creaked.

He ran to the hallway and up the stairs, his long legs

taking them three at a time. He was in time to see a door closing ahead of him and hear a key turning in the lock. He approached it boldly, his lean wolfish face wearing a hungry expression. Raising his claw, he knocked on the bedroom door.

"Little pig, little pig, let me come in."

A shot rang out and Carter flinched as a bullet punched through the door and went sailing past his cheek.

Carter stepped back and gave the door a mighty kick with the flat of his foot. The wood splintered around the lock and Carter burst into the room, throwing himself to one side to avoid a second bullet.

Confronting him was a matronly woman with a proud bosom, a strong face and a service revolver. She was actually quite admirable, Carter thought. He had very little time for hysterics or fainting fits, and there was none of that here. This was a woman of character. And wealth. The diamonds around her neck were clearly worth a king's ransom. But he hadn't come to her house for something as trivial as the contents of her jewellery box.

She cracked off another shot, but Carter had anticipated it and flung himself out of the way, taking refuge behind the huge bed. He had spent most of his life around guns and he could spot the signs when someone was about to fire. From his vantage point he watched as the woman shifted her shoulder to balance the revolver in her outstretched hands; guns were heavier than most people imagined. Then he observed the movement in the muscles around her shoulders, then down her arm to her trigger finger…

The fourth shot struck the wall harmlessly behind him.

Carter reached for his own weapon, which was slung across his back, and prepared to return fire. It was a length of hollow hardwood, just over two feet long. Carter had seen these blowpipes used to great effect during his travels in South America. Careful not to touch its tip, Carter inserted the poison dart into the pipe and lifted it to his lips. He had prepared the *curare* himself, from plant extracts gathered on the banks of the great Orinoco river. In the right proportions, the poison would act as a muscle relaxant, knocking his victim unconscious in seconds. Of course, if the proportions were wrong it would kill her stone dead.

He inflated his cheeks and gave a single hard puff, just as he had been taught by a Jakaltek huntsman he had lived with for a while in the foothills of the Cuchumatanes Mountains. The dart flew straight and true, hitting the woman in the exposed skin of her neck. Within moments the poison was flooding through the woman's system. She staggered, fired again, then collapsed to the ground in an ungainly heap.

Carter went to her side and, picking up her limp wrist, he checked her pulse. It was fluctuating wildly, as he expected, but as he continued to hold her it began to find a more steady rhythm. Carter smiled and then hoisted the woman up over his shoulder. He grunted slightly as he took her weight; she was quite sturdy for her size.

Let's see who's the clever one now, Mr. Sweet, he thought as he carried the woman away.

Her Majesty Victoria, by the Grace of God, of the United Kingdom of Great Britain and Ireland Queen, Defender of the Faith, Empress of India, was running. Or, as close to running as a rather small, rather fat monarch of the realm ever got. She lifted her huge skirts in her small pink hands and scuttled after Mr. Sweet.

"Mr. Sweet!" she called after him. "Slow down. Prime Minister!"

"No, Your Majesty," Sweet replied in a tone which brooked no argument. "The carriage is waiting and you must leave for the safety of Balmoral immediately!"

"But, Prime Minister," she persisted, "how can I leave London in her hour of need?"

Mr. Sweet halted in his tracks, his boots squeaking on the marble floor. He turned on her, his face red. "There is madness beyond the gates of Buckingham Palace! There is rioting in the streets! You will not be serving your subjects by putting your own life in danger." He took her hand firmly. "Now be a good queen and get in the carriage!"

Outside the palace, Queen Victoria was met by a wall of fog so dense that she could barely see her hand when she extended her arm. She was surrounded on all sides by her household staff, their faces showing the same mixture of fear and grim resolve.

"This way, Ma'am," said an officer, offering his hand, and leading her to the waiting carriage. Queen Victoria mounted the step and then hesitated.

There was something wrong here, she sensed, more than just the strange mist and the new Prime Minister's rude manner.

This was not her usual carriage. Nor was it her usual carriage driver, waiting up front with whip in hand…

"Quickly," Sweet bellowed. "Get in the carriage now!"

"One is not in the habit of being dictated to by one's subjects," the Queen retorted. She looked again at the faces of her servants and followed the line of their gaze… finding the reason for their horror in the rank of hooded figures watching over them with rifles held level.

Sweet stormed towards the Queen and shoved her backwards with both hands.

"Get in now, you old sow," he growled.

The Queen toppled backwards and, before she could scramble to her feet, she heard the bolts slamming into place on the carriage door, a steel shutter sliding down simultaneously, blocking the window and any thought of escape.

"Release me now," she shouted.

Sweet didn't reply. But Queen Victoria had her answer in the deafening volley of shots that rang out.

She felt the coach sink on its suspension as the hooded figures took up their positions on all sides and then, with a jerk, the wheels began to turn as the horses led the carriage out of the gates of Buckingham Palace and away.

CHAPTER 15

KILL OR BE KILLED

The Watchers stood silently in the belfry of St Mary-le-Bow and listened to the sounds of a city destroying itself. In the East End it was said that if you were born within the sound of these Bow bells then you were a true Cockney. It was sad, Ben thought, that if you were anywhere within the sound of the Bow bells now, it probably meant that your life was falling apart around you.

Mother Shepherd had summoned them and her expression was grave. "This is the worst day I have ever seen," she began. "These are the worst words that I have ever spoken…"

Ben held his breath. Mother Shepherd was old and she was beautiful, but there was flint in her voice.

"The Legion are only days away from taking control of London, possibly Great Britain."

Ben gasped. "But what about the Queen?" he said. "Old Vic won't take it lying down."

"Queen Victoria has been kidnapped," said Mother Shepherd. "Mr. Sweet has also removed the Prime Minister and taken his place. Our spy in the Under has told us that Sweet has also removed the other six members of the Council of Seven."

"So Sweet is the only one pulling the strings in the Legion, then," said Ben.

Mother Shepherd nodded. "I had always hoped that it would not come to this," she continued. "But as of now, we must consider ourselves at war. The Watcher way is that of peace, but the prospect of our nation under Legion rule is too terrible to contemplate. We have no choice...we must rise up in defiance."

"Kill or be killed," said Jago Moon, scrubbing his hand over his stubbled head.

"I did not say that, my old friend," said Mother Shepherd. "Violence is still the act of a coward, but we *shall* defend ourselves and the innocent. We *will* place ourselves in harm's way to save the lives of strangers.

The Watchers will be the breakwater against this tide of hatred. We *still* do not aim to kill…we want to *stop* the Legion, but I think we all know that some lives will be lost."

"On both sides," said Ben.

A howl issued from Josiah's lips, a cry of sadness and regret that erupted with such force it almost tore the air around it. This was the mighty warrior angel as Ben had first met him, the Weeping Man; full of sadness at the foolish ways of men.

"There is more," said Josiah. "In three days' time, when the clock tolls midnight, and the twelfth of March becomes the thirteenth, the Feast of Ravens will begin. That is the night when the powers of darkness are at their most potent. The Legion believe that if there is a coronation on that black night in conjunction with a sacrifice, if someone is mad or foolish or wicked enough to place the Crown of Corruption on their head, then it would herald a reign without end."

"Although the Watchers have done their best over the centuries to hide the thirty coins of Judas and scatter them to the four corners of the globe, the Legion have tracked them all down. All but one, that is," said Mother Shepherd pointedly. "If we can keep that last foul Coin out of their grasp, then the Crown – their great weapon – will remain incomplete. It will *still* be capable of unimaginable evil and destruction, but we will, at least, have a chance of defeating Sweet and the Legion."

Ben shifted uncomfortably, the Coin like a burning coal in his pocket.

"You said Sweet needed a sacrifice," said Ben.

Josiah and Mother Shepherd exchanged glances.

"There's no easy way to tell you, Ben…but our spy thinks that the intended victim is your brother, Nathaniel."

"Over my dead body!" Ben snapped. "If they hurt Nathaniel, I'll…" His fingertips brushed the Coin in his pocket and Ben found his thoughts were trapped in an angry world of red.

"Benjamin," said Mother Shepherd. "Look at me!"

There was something about her voice that pierced through Ben's rage. He guiltily let the Coin fall back, and felt its influence receding.

"We *know* that you can stop the Legion, Ben," she said, her own voice level and soothing. "And we *will* save your brother."

Part of Ben wanted to give her the Coin then, be shot of the damned thing. And yet… And yet…why not keep hold of it, for just a little while longer? It was safer with him, wasn't it? It made him feel so strong, after all.

"Does the spy know where Nathaniel is being held?" said Ben.

"I'm sorry, Ben," said Moon. "He did at first, but apparently Sweet keeps moving him. All we know is that the Feast is going to be held at the Tower of London."

"So we'd better tear the city apart to find him," said Ben. "Who's with me?" he asked, walking away without waiting for a reply.

"He *is* the Hand of Heaven," said Mother Shepherd, when she and Josiah were alone in the belfry. "I can see the leader rising up in him already."

"Is that why you haven't taken the Coin from him?" Josiah asked.

Mother Shepherd paused, taken aback. "How long have you known that Ben has it?"

"All along," Josiah replied. "The same as you."

"Do you think that anyone else suspects?"

"Not in the Watchers, no." Josiah smiled. "I think they mostly put his temperament down to his red hair."

"Do you think I've been foolish to let him hang on to it?"

"Not foolish," said Josiah, "but maybe not wise."

"If I take the Coin from him – if *you* take the Coin from

him – then its hold on Ben will remain as strong as ever; he will always yearn for it, like a drunkard for the bottle. But *when* he gives it up of his own accord, that will be the moment when the power of temptation is broken. Then we will know that he has accepted his destiny."

Josiah nodded. "Let's hope he makes that choice soon."

"And you promise not to intervene before then?"

"Not unless it becomes absolutely necessary," Josiah agreed. He looked up at the dark sky. "I must leave you now, good Mother, I have a family matter to attend to."

"Godspeed," said Mother Shepherd and Josiah walked away.

Left alone, Mother Shepherd gazed out over the stricken city. "Oh Benjamin," she breathed softly. "Please find the strength inside to do the right thing… Please prove that I'm right to have placed all our lives in your hands."

CHAPTER 16

NO MORE TEARS

The Weeping Man reached the edge of the roof and threw himself into the embrace of the air, his wings emerging from the slits in his coat and carrying him high up above the grasp of the smog and smoke. Since he had been called to aid the Watchers he had lived among them and done his best to fit in. He had worn their clothes and eaten their food. And he had spent most of the time on his feet. But the air was his natural element. He was an angel, a servant of the Uncreated One, and he was born for the skies.

Part of him felt a pang of guilt as he enjoyed the rush of wind beneath his wings. By necessity Josiah kept his true form hidden most of the time, but this blanket of fog, which had brought such misery to thousands, allowed him the brief opportunity to soar openly without fear of being seen from the ground. However, he had not left Mother Shepherd simply in pursuit of pleasure; Josiah was searching for another angel, someone he had known a lifetime ago in a different realm.

Back then his name had been Moloch, but now he had chosen a new title for himself.

Josiah was hunting for the Nightmare Child.

Giggling, the Nightmare Child skipped through the streets of London.

In the fog he met a woman, afraid and lost. He smiled at her and showed her her children, struggling beneath a swarm of beetles. He let himself into a grand house where he amused himself by picking out a tune on the piano, making sure that he was never seen by the lady of the house, of course. Playing the same keys over and over, until the poor confused woman knew his song by heart. He left her, sitting in the corner of the music room with her knees drawn up to her chest while she rocked back and forth, singing the tune to herself.

No two nightmares were exactly the same. He was the

creaking on the stairs, the tapping on the windowpane, the turning of the door handle. He was the shadow that moved on its own, the face with no mouth, the undertaker who nailed the coffin lid down in spite of the shouts from inside.

Nathaniel Kingdom's nightmare had been especially delicious. It involved his brother Benjamin and a wall built between them that Nathaniel desperately tried to tear down, scrabbling at the stonework until his fingers were raw.

Nathaniel struggled for such a long time before he finally gave in to the madness. It had been glorious; the boy's fear had tasted so sweet.

The Nightmare Child grinned. This was quite his favourite game and he wouldn't stop until all of London had joined in the fun.

Where to play next? he wondered. And then an idea struck him that was so delightful that he clapped his little hands.

It was time for a prison visit.

Josiah found the Nightmare Child easily enough – he followed the sounds of distress.

The ancient being was sitting cross-legged on the wall

of Holloway Prison. Josiah circled twice and then landed beside him.

The Nightmare Child smiled at him as he arrived. It was a sickening sneer.

"I don't know why you bothered to bring that," said the Nightmare Child, his eyes on Josiah's sword. "You and I both know that you won't use it."

Josiah said nothing.

"It has been such a beautiful day, Josiah," said the Nightmare Child, giving a wistful sigh. "Such larks. I'm so glad you could join me. Why not have a seat?" He peered down into the prison yard. "I think you're in time to see something special."

But Josiah did not sit; instead he crouched on his haunches, ready to launch himself into the air at a moment's notice. He knew Moloch well enough not to let his guard down for a moment.

"Moloch," he addressed the fallen angel, "I wish we did not have to meet under these circumstances."

"Circumstances? Whatever do you mean?" Beneath them, under the choking fog, came the sounds of a prison in full riot. "I've only been making a few house calls," the Nightmare Child said, smiling. "These human minds are so fragile, I find, so open to suggestion." Wails of torment echoed up to greet them. "I think I might fly down later on and open the gates, just to see what happens. I never did approve of prisons."

"Which is a shame, considering where you will be going one day," said Josiah, with flint in his voice.

"And you'll be there to bind the eternal chains around me I suppose, brother dear."

"I am ashamed to be called by that name," Josiah replied.

"I'm hurt," said Moloch. "But the fact remains, you *are* my brother."

"Not since you left our home and followed the Burning Man."

"Picky, picky," Moloch scoffed. "You always were the sensitive one. What is that name they've given you while you walk among them? The Weeping Man? You're not going to cry now, are you?"

"There's no weakness in compassion," Josiah countered.

"Really?" The Nightmare Child filled his voice with mock amazement. "I can pick any one of these pitiful humans and if I threaten to hurt them I can make you jump around like a puppet trying to save them. Are you telling me that doesn't make you weak?"

"Why do you hate them so much?"

"Why do you care for them at all?" Moloch snapped back.

"I care for them because the Uncreated One cares for them. I don't need any other reason."

"But their lives are so short and insignificant, their ambitions so limited." He sounded incredulous. "Why should *anyone* be troubled if they live or die?"

"Tread carefully," Josiah warned. "You know that if I ask it, I could have an army of the angelic host join me now and we could sweep you and the Legion into the sea."

"Ha! We both know that is an empty threat. The Uncreated One will *never* allow the host to swoop in and save the day. He likes these humans to solve their own problems. You, dear brother, are all they have."

"You're forgetting about the Hand of Heaven."

"What? That red-headed boy? He'll be the Hand of Hell before the Feast of Ravens, take my word for it."

Josiah locked the Nightmare Child in his gaze and rose slowly to his feet. "I hoped that you might see the error of your ways, but I realize now that you are beyond redemption."

The Nightmare Child hissed, his face twisted with rage. "Redemption? Why should I want that? In three days' time you will bow down to me!" he said, his own wings unfurling and carrying him into the air.

"I pity you," said Josiah as he flew away. "But I won't shed a tear for you."

CHAPTER 17

PARAFFIN
AND MATCHES

Ben's plan was simple enough: find some filthy Legionnaires and make them tell him where Nathaniel was being held. There was nothing more that he could do on the Liberator – that was down to his pa and the engineers now – leaving Ben and his party free to hunt.

Shouldering a fresh pack of Watcher supplies, Ben stood close to Jago Moon, with Lucy and Ghost. He knew that the old man's keen ears were straining, picking up every nuance and vibration in the air around them, each movement of furtive feet, each whispered breath.

"This way," he rasped. "Stay close to old Jago Moon and you won't go far wrong." Obediently the young

Watchers fell in behind him and let the blind man lead the way.

His ears were searching for the telltale sounds which would alert him to the presence of the Legion. The Legion moved invisibly in tunnels beneath the pavements, but that did not mean that they couldn't be heard when they were near enough to the surface. Moon had trained himself to pick out the echoes of subterranean footfalls, often accompanied by muted whispers. Next he would listen for the clang of a ladder being climbed, the creak of a trapdoor or the rasp of a metal cover being slid aside. Then the quality of the voices would change, from the muffled reverberation of the tunnel to the free resonance of the open air. Plus, Legionnaires would often give themselves away by muttering things about "Watcher scum" – that was always a good hint.

They didn't have long to wait before they found what they were searching for.

Moon's ears pricked up and his nose twitched in alarm. The harsh tang of paraffin. The chime of glass bottles, rattling together in a crate. The whisper of dark intent.

The rasp of a phosphor match being struck.

"Fire starters!"

Mickelwhite struck the match and lit the rag. Bedlam picked up the bottle filled with paraffin and hurled it against the side of the warehouse. Jimmy Dips held the crate. Hans Schulman kept watch.

They all wore thick woollen cowls that had been issued to them by the Quartermaster, the Legion's notorious weaponsmith, and for an instant their shadowy faces were illuminated by the blossom of fire. They cheered as another bottle shattered against the wall, the huge splash of flames quickly feeding on the timbers. They felt the warmth of the flames on their faces – it felt good.

"Right," said Mickelwhite, "we can't hang around here, gentlemen – you know Mr. Sweet's instructions."

"But why?" asked Jimmy Dips. "I mean, it's fun, scaring people an' that. But what does the Legion get out of it?"

Mickelwhite explained slowly, as if he were talking to an idiot. "Because what the Legion desires more than anything else is to be feared. Because when people are afraid of you they will do what you tell them to do."

Jimmy Dips still looked at him blankly. "And how does that help us?"

"The Legion aren't going to hide for much longer, Jimmy. Don't you get it? It was never going to be about us simply choosing to live outside of the law. The plan was always that one day *we* would start *making* the laws.

After the Feast of Ravens, that's exactly what's going to happen."

"But how are we going to do that, Captain?" said Jimmy.

"Over my dead body!" an unexpected voice thundered, as Jago Moon charged at them.

The old man was terribly quick. A single roundhouse kick knocked Hans Schulman flying into Jimmy Dips, sending the crate of paraffin bombs clattering to the ground. The bottles shattered on the cobbles, the broken glass glistening like scattered jewels in the light of the flames.

Meanwhile, the stealthy, silent Watcher with a shaven head, the one they called "the Mute", was walking rings round Bedlam. Mickelwhite watched out of the corner of his eye. Every time Bedlam launched one of his kicks or big swinging punches, the Watcher simply ducked beneath it or flicked it out of the way, and then countered with a short sharp punch of his own.

Jimmy Dips was meant to be Mickelwhite's squire, and as such he was supposed to rush to fight alongside him at times like this. However, Mickelwhite could see that Jimmy was far too occupied trying not to get himself beaten up by the Watcher girl they all knew as "Scarface".

Through the swirls of mist Mickelwhite's eyes settled on the fourth Watcher in the group and he smiled as he pulled his sabre from its scabbard.

"Ben Kingdom! You're mine!" he shouted and charged towards him.

Kingdom reacted far quicker than he had expected, easily ducking beneath his sabre slash and then drawing a sword of his own from a sheath slung across his back.

"This will be fun," Mickelwhite declared. Not waiting another moment, he lashed out towards Ben's head, his sword missing by a whisper. Ben was not slow to respond however, planting a straight-legged kick in Mickelwhite's stomach, his own blade licking out towards the captain's cheek.

Winded, Mickelwhite staggered backwards, bringing up his blade just in time to save himself.

Noticing that the broken crate was now behind Ben, he launched a series of hacking blows designed to force the boy backwards in an attempt to make him fall. Ben blocked every slash that Mickelwhite rained upon him, but he stumbled as the back of his legs met the wooden box and his feet flew out from beneath him on the paraffin-slick cobbles. Ben hit the ground heavily, but before Mickelwhite could follow through, Ben sprang up from his prone position to land upright in a single fluid move.

"Tell me where my brother is," said Ben, "or I'm going to kick you all the way to Whitechapel."

Mickelwhite circled him warily. "Oh, you'd like that, wouldn't you? Is that why you're here? On some errand for the Witch Queen of Spies?"

Ben made a darting jab with his sword, narrowly missing Mickelwhite's shoulder. "Say that again," he warned through clenched teeth.

"What name would you prefer me to use, I wonder?" mused Mickelwhite. "*Hag?*"

"Her name is Mother Shepherd," said Ben, "and if you insult her again, I swear—"

"How about *Harpy*?"

Ben appeared to be battling with his emotions. "I'm a Watcher," he said, "I don't want to hurt you..."

"*Crone.*"

"Tell me where my brother is and I'll let you walk away..."

"*Harridan.*"

"I'm telling you, don't push me..."

"*WITCH!*"

Ben's face contorted as he succumbed to his rage. Mickelwhite rammed his advantage home, his sabre slicing the air. Ben flicked out a scissor kick as he dodged the slashing blade, but his anger had thrown his timing.

Mickelwhite was able to evade it easily, moving in with a quick savage elbow that caught Ben across the throat and dropped him to the ground. Ben was still clutching the sword in his hand, but Mickelwhite brought a stop to that with a sharp stamp across his fingers. Ben relinquished his grip and Mickelwhite kicked the blade away. Then he stood over Ben in triumph, the tip of his blade resting against the other boy's neck.

"I'm going to enjoy this," he said.

Without warning, something hit Mickelwhite hard in the pit of his stomach, bending him double. Grimacing through the pain, Mickelwhite raised his eyes to see the Mute smiling at him over his levelled crossbow pistol. The bolt that was aimed at him had a padded head rather than an arrow tip, the same as the one that had just hit him, Mickelwhite noted gratefully, but he still had to be careful.

He looked around for the rest of his brigade.

He found Jimmy Dips flat on his back. Scarface was standing with one foot on his chest, smiling alarmingly. Bedlam was rolling on the ground, holding his nose, and Schulman was missing, presumably being pursued by Jago Moon.

"You have me at a disadvantage," the captain conceded. "Jimmy, Bedlam," he called out, "it's time to stop playing and say goodbye." He placed his own weapon on the ground and raised his hands in the air. "You Watchers wouldn't shoot an unarmed man, would you?"

Ghost lowered his bow, and Scarface stepped away from Dips as Ben stood up.

"That is precisely why you will lose this war," Mickelwhite sneered, as Dips and Bedlam limped over to his side. "Your precious morals make you weak."

"Tell me where Nathaniel is!" Ben demanded.

"Or what?" said Mickelwhite. "You'll shoot me again with one of your padded arrows? Please."

Mickelwhite was vaguely aware that Ben was fiddling with something in his pocket. As he watched, Ben's lips twisted into a snarl of frustration and rage. Then, before Mickelwhite could react, Ben lunged for him and he fell back beneath the hammering of Ben's fists.

"Tell! Me! Where! My! Brother! Is!" spat Ben, each word punctuated by a punch.

Mickelwhite felt a heavy smack to the side of his head; a forceful uppercut that caught him hard under the ribs. He struggled beneath Ben, but the full force of the boy's weight, and his sudden fury, pinned Mickelwhite to the ground. It was all that he could do to shield his head from the rain of relentless blows.

In the end it was Moon who dragged Ben away, still snarling.

Mickelwhite struggled to his feet, aching and dazed from the assault. He tried to regain his composure by brushing himself down but his fingers were trembling too much to pull off the act. He turned and led his brigade away at a run.

"I will find Nathaniel!" Ben shouted at their retreating backs. "And when I do, I won't need those Watcher rules any more. Then I'll be back to finish you!"

CHAPTER 18

READY, AIM, FIRE!

Claw Carter left the Under and retired to his sanctum, his suite of rooms beneath the British Museum. He clicked shut the iron maiden which acted as a hidden door and looked around. He was greeted by treasures collected from the four corners of the globe and skeletons in glass cabinets. But not by anything living.

Wearily he shrugged off his leather coat and hung it on its stand. He turned up the gas lamps and went to sit at his desk in the welcoming arms of his chair. Inevitably his eyes were pulled to the desk drawer. It was locked and he firmly intended to keep it that way. *Not tonight, James,* he told himself and he rose from his chair in a deliberate effort to distance himself from the temptation of looking inside. By means of a distraction, he walked around and examined some of the artefacts he had amassed, all the while fighting back the urge to take the key from his watch chain and slip it into the beckoning lock.

A skull stared back at him from its plinth. It was a beautiful object, in Carter's opinion. It had been dipped in gold by its previous owner and it shone luxuriously. Two fat rubies sat in the eye sockets and seemed to wink at him. It was an authentic temple skull from the Pyramid of the Moon at Teotihuacan, with original red crusting around the teeth. It would have been a crime against archaeology to wash an Aztec blood cup too thoroughly, he thought.

Claw Carter smiled at the memory. Notwithstanding the arduous trek, the treacherous guides and the Goliath bird-eating spiders that invaded the camp, it had been a happy time. Before the Legion.

Before the locked drawer.

A muffled moan from the other side of his room snapped Carter out of his reminiscences. The sound was coming from the sarcophagus that stood in the corner. Carter turned and walked over to it, unperturbed; his guest had been bound to wake up at some point.

"Mrs. Sweet, oh Mrs. Sweet," he sing-songed. Inside

the Egyptian casket, Honoraria Sweet began to make muffled threats through her gag. Carter banged his fist down hard on the cabinet. "Shut up and sit tight," he ordered, "I'm trying to plot your son's murder out here."

The woman began to bellow and Carter walked away; he found it a very annoying noise.

It really had been so easy to capture Sweet's mother; no challenge at all for a man of his talents.

A man of his talents... He rolled the phrase around in his mind. Such a man needed to inspire the next generation if he was to have any legacy at all. But who in the world could he give the benefit of his wisdom to? None of the guttersnipes in the Legion seemed even remotely worthy.

Where was the son for him to shape in his own image?

The question was left hanging and unanswered in the air.

Night had fallen with a vengeance, the darkness only lifted by the light of burning buildings in the East End. Mr. Sweet raised his voice to address the troops, the Coldstream Regiment of Foot Guards, stationed at their barracks in Windsor. They were *his* to command, he realized with satisfaction. He admired the ranks as they stood proudly to attention, resplendent in their red tunics and bearskins.

Fiercely loyal to Queen and country, Mr. Sweet was well aware that these men would be appalled if they knew that they were being used to further his own ambitions. However, Mr. Sweet stood before them as the Prime Minister of Her Majesty's Government. They would obey his commands without question. And if any found themselves troubled by their conscience? Well, soon he would have the Crown of Corruption and he would *make* them yield.

"London has fallen into the hands of looters and thugs," said Sweet, "and in order to restore calm to the city I have declared a curfew which you shall be enforcing. Anyone found on the streets before oh-six hundred hours and after twenty-one hundred hours can be presumed to be a threat to the peace and as such are to be forcibly detained. A body of men is setting up an enclosed camp in St. James's Park where these villains can be imprisoned.

"If you are met with any resistance, you are authorized to fire at will. I expect the whole of London to be firmly under military control within the next forty-eight hours." *In time for the Feast of Ravens. In time for my moment of triumph.*

"Furthermore, I have been made aware that there is a group of anarchists who are using this blasted fog and the current breakdown in law and order to further their despicable ends. This rebellious organization calls itself 'The Watchers'. You can recognize a Watcher by the uniform they wear."

Beside Mr. Sweet was a large easel covered in a black cloth. He now drew the covering aside to reveal an artist's sketch. "Observe the long leather coat, sometimes criss-crossed with belts and packs. Notice the brass goggles they use to hide their identities, and the scarf covering the mouth. See, too, the sturdy boots." Sweet pointed all these features out with his swagger stick.

"The Watchers are dangerous individuals. They are enemies of the state. If you see any individual wearing a uniform such as this…" He smoothed his moustache with deep satisfaction. "You are to shoot on sight!"

DAY FOUR
11TH MARCH, 1892

CHAPTER 19

THE BEGINNING OF THE END

The fog was winning.

The *Legion* were winning, Ben realized as he woke from a troubled sleep.

Ben felt ashamed of himself. Something inside had snapped when Mickelwhite mocked the Watchers. Part of Ben's fury had been born out of the need to find Nathaniel, part of it had been fuelled by the Coin's insidious influence, Ben knew full well. But the *worst* part was the one that had agreed with Mickelwhite.

Ben loved the Watchers, but sometimes they were like toothless lions. For a boy who had grown up with the rough and tumble of Old Gravel Lane, Ben struggled with the moral code that Mickelwhite had ridiculed. It might be alright for "Cowpat" Cowper, his old Sunday school teacher, but it wasn't much use to Ben.

Pushing those thoughts down, Ben looked out across the city with bleary eyes. Huge clouds of fog had turned black and glowed red from within. At Mother Shepherd's command, the Watchers had made camp on the roof of St Bartholomew's Hospital, and the wounded and scared had been joining them in droves. The fires kept burning and the refugees kept coming. The Watchers were pushed to their very limits. They continued now through sheer determination and willpower alone. There were too many people to help. Not enough blankets. Not enough food. Not enough time. Tempers were growing frayed. Nerves stretched taut. And still the fog grew.

The whole of the roof was a mass of huddled bodies, every man jack of them as drained as Ben was. Scattered across the city, he could make out a dozen other islands like theirs emerging through the fog, where the Watchers had set up makeshift shelters for the refugees, using canvas tents, tarpaulins, rope and whatever meagre supplies came to hand. He knew that this was what the Watchers had been doing in secret for years; picking up the pieces of a broken world.

The one small consolation for the Watchers was that

because no one on the ground could even see their own front door any more, let alone what was happening above their heads, it allowed the Watchers to fix in place temporarily the ladders, planks and zip wires which they were usually so careful to pull up from prying eyes. Ben and some of the other lads had spent hours yesterday setting up a network of sorts and opening up a handful of the main runs across the rooftops.

His pa had still been working on the Liberator when Ben's eyes had finally shut some time between two and three in the morning. However, this morning he had vanished and Ben guessed that he had set off before dawn to siphon gas from the giant gasometers at King's Cross – another vital component of the machine. It was certainly looking impressive, Ben thought, although it was still some way from being ready. The hull was finished and the decking, silk work and rigging were nearly complete. But the most technical elements – those involving the stolen gas and the steam engine – could not be rushed. It was dangerous work and the last thing they needed was an explosion. In Ben's mind, the Liberator could *still* play a vital role in defeating the Legion, or hindering them at least. If only the Feast of Ravens wasn't two short days away.

Ben massaged his neck in an effort to make himself feel more human. He experimented with his new hat, setting it slightly further back on his head and tilted to the left; a black boat on his sea of red hair. He spotted Lucy at the far end of the roof, handing out steaming mugs of tea. He waved to her and their eyes met. Lucy looked exhausted but she gave a brave smile and Ben imagined that it was just for him.

Ben sluiced his face in half a cup of water, made an effort to clean his teeth by chewing on some liquorice root, then turned up the collar on his long Watcher coat so it looked suitably stylish. He found Ghost sitting by one of the breakfast fires, making some toast from stale bread and sharing it out.

"'Allo, mate," said Ben. "Any idea where I'll find Mother this morning?"

Ghost pointed over the fog to the dome of St Paul's.

"You have to admire her," said Ben, as he set off to speak to her. "The old girl's got some style."

The planks and ladders which spanned the gaps between the buildings gave Ben the feeling that he was running through the clouds. He found Mother Shepherd easily enough, standing serenely on the Stone Gallery which ran round the base of Sir Christopher Wren's great dome.

"Come over here," she called to him, when she saw him clamber up onto the rail. "It's chilly this morning; give an old woman a hug."

After a moment's hesitation, Ben put his arms around Mother Shepherd's shoulders. He stood there stiffly for a second, and then he began to melt. She may have been small, but there was a strength inside Mother Shepherd that Ben would have pitched against a bare-knuckle boxer any day of the week. He needed this, Ben realized: the acceptance, the love. That was what the Legion could never offer him and would never understand.

It was Mother Shepherd who broke off first. "Benjamin," she said kindly. "I *know* that you have been struggling, Brother Moon told me how you…went too far when you met that Legionnaire…" Ben felt his face flush red, both with embarrassment and the stirrings of anger. "But," she continued, "I think I understand *why*."

"Because I'm not good enough to be a Watcher," Ben replied bluntly.

"No, Benjamin," she corrected. "You must never think that."

"So why then?" Ben snapped, hating himself for being rude but not able to stop.

"I made a mistake," said Mother Shepherd. "Can you forgive me?"

Ben looked back at her quizzically.

"It's *my* fault that you feel the way you do, Ben," she went on. "Josiah wanted to warn you of the danger earlier, but I thought that because of your destiny, because you are the Hand of Heaven, its dark power wouldn't be able to touch you and the Watchers would be safer if you carried the burden for us all... It was selfish of me, I can see that now." Mother Shepherd appeared older then than Ben had ever seen her, a great sadness clouding her face. "I'm so sorry for all the pain I've caused you."

She looked him straight in the eye. "Why don't you give it to me, Benjamin?" she said. "It must be so heavy, won't you let me take the load instead?"

"What are you talking about?" said Ben, feeling the blood drain from his face as his deepest secret was laid out in the open.

"I've known you had it since the battle of Tower Bridge, Ben, but I trusted you – I *still* trust you – and I was hoping that you would decide to give it up voluntarily when the time was right. But everything has got out of control." She shook her head. "This evil fog, the fires, everything... It's too much for us... We can't wait for you to be rid of it on your own accord. We need you to be free of it now."

"I don't know what you mean," said Ben, his hands beginning to clench and unclench with emotion. His left hand in particular started to throb with angry power.

"Benjamin," said Mother Shepherd, still displaying infinite patience, which for some reason Ben found infuriating, "sometimes there are things that we want which can only do us harm. It is a parent's job to try and steer their children away from the things that will hurt them."

"You're not my mother."

"And I'm not trying to replace her, Benjamin. Yet I want you to know that I love you just as if you were my own."

Ben's heart lurched inside him. He wanted this. He wanted this love and acceptance that had been missing from his life for so long.

But the Coin wouldn't let him have it.

"Just leave me alone!" he shouted in her face. "I can solve this by myself. I don't need your help!" His voice cracked with anger and the veins were standing proud all down his left arm.

"The Coin in your pocket is the last of the Thirty, Ben," said Mother Shepherd. "The most evil, the most powerful, the most destructive of them all." She extended her hand, still speaking in her gentle tone. "*I* made the mistakes, Benjamin; *me*, not *you*. I can't bear to see you so troubled. Let me carry the Coin from here."

"It's *my* Coin!"

"No, Benjamin, the Coin owns you, not the other way round. Please just give it to me."

Mother Shepherd took a step nearer and Ben could feel

his left arm rising, as if to strike her. He stopped himself and retreated round the walkway. "Please get away from me, Mother Shepherd, I don't want to hurt you."

"See," she said. "There's your heart shining through. Just let me take the Coin and then we can go and get some breakfast."

"*NOOOOO!*" said Ben, and this time his voice was a roar. His left hand was tremulous and possessed of a strength that was not his own. "The Coin is mine!" he bellowed and brought his left fist down on the stone railing, smashing the masonry in two.

Time stopped.

A crack raced through the stonework towards Mother Shepherd.

She was standing with her hand on the balustrade, the carved stone wall which kept people safe from the drop. The impact of Ben's left fist had shattered the stonework in front of him, and the damage was radiating outwards at an alarming rate. Fissures began to open in the stone walkway that they were standing on. A spider's web at first; thin, delicate lines of damage. Then deep, black scorelines through the stone.

"No!" Ben called, in panic this time, as all his anger dissipated. "You can have the Coin, I don't want it. Take it, please!"

But as quick as his change of heart was, the cracks were quicker. He could feel the shifting of the stone beneath his feet like breaking ice, the fractured plates sliding underneath him as he tried to adjust his weight. The fault lines raced towards Mother Shepherd, splintering through the platform as the balustrade fell away in chunks.

Mother Shepherd was old. She was slow. And she didn't stand a chance.

Ben saw her stagger and fall and he put everything into a dive, throwing himself towards her disappearing form. He skidded on his belly as he stretched his hands out towards her, even while the stone continued to fracture and disintegrate around them. By some miracle Ben managed to grab hold of Mother Shepherd's wrist. She was hardly as heavy as a child and it came as a shock to Ben how fragile she really was.

Ignoring the pain in his own muscles, Ben started to drag her back up. "Hold on," he said, his teeth clenched with the effort. "I'll pull you up."

The old lady hung perilously beneath him. Ben could feel her bones through the thin tissue of her skin. His hands were wet with perspiration and his arms felt as if they might pop from his shoulders at any second.

"Try to reach me with your other hand," he urged. "I can do this."

"No," she replied gently, her expression a picture of serenity.

"Please let me try," said Ben, a tear tracing a line down his cheek even as his grip continued to slip.

"Let me go, Benjamin," said Mother Shepherd, no trace of either fear or condemnation in her voice. "There's no sense in us both dying. I'm ready for my future…and you're ready for yours."

"No," said Ben. "I can't let you go. I won't."

"I love you, Benjamin Kingdom. I know you'll make me proud."

And as the tears rushed to Ben's eyes, the stone beneath them gave another mighty lurch, and Mother Shepherd disappeared into the fog amongst a storm of falling rubble.

CHAPTER 20

A DEATH IN THE FAMILY

Please don't be dead. Please don't be dead. Please don't be dead.

Ben said the words over and over, as if by repeating them he could keep Mother Shepherd alive.

He couldn't take in what his eyes had just witnessed.

His mind could not accept what his left hand had caused.

But he couldn't deny that he was about to fall too.

Ben considered simply letting go, to rid the Watchers of his menace once and for all. But he dismissed that thought just as quickly; he couldn't know peace until his brother was free.

Ben quickly whipped his grappling hook from his belt and secured it to what remained of the balustrade, then he clung to the rope with both hands and kicked out with his feet. Part abseiling, part falling, Ben chased Mother Shepherd towards the ground. His hands burning as the rope stripped the skin from his palms, he recklessly dropped through the hungry fog at breakneck speed.

The mist was so thick that Ben had no real way of knowing how far away the ground was. Or what would be waiting for him when he got there.

Please don't be dead. Please don't be dead. Please don't be dead.

Jago Moon was never far from Mother Shepherd. Although she had not given him the job officially, he considered himself to be her bodyguard.

Whenever she went away to pray, even when she insisted on solitude, he always followed her in secret, relying on his own stealth to keep him hidden. Some men might curse their blindness, and the fact that they could never look at a pretty girl again, but in a strange way Jago Moon's lack of sight allowed him to paint a perfect picture of Mother Shepherd. He knew that she was as old as he was. He had touched her skin and felt the soft folds of wrinkles. But in his mind's eye he saw her as about eighteen, the same age as he saw himself until his joints ached and reminded him of the truth.

He could not see the fog that had stolen London, but he could feel its presence in the cold clamminess that surrounded him, probing his flesh with its searching fingers. His keen ears could hear the fog too, or at least they could recognize how it muffled and dampened the sounds of the street. There was still so much panic. Some people had been wandering for days, hopelessly lost and brimming over with despair. Then there were those Legion yobs, hell-bent on adding to the terror. *Let one of them come my way*, thought Moon, his hand itching to pull his sword from its hiding place in his cane.

Mother Shepherd was out of harm's way at least, he consoled himself. Where could be safer for a Watcher than St Paul's? High up over the city, that was where the Watchers were always best protected. A smile crossed his lips as he thought of Mother Shepherd, as aged as she was, still nimble enough to cross a death slide or climb a rope ladder.

Suddenly a vibration above his head shook Jago Moon from his reveries. It was a rattle at first, like a sudden hail shower on a spring day. But then it was followed by the thunder of something breaking and as the rain of stones became heavier, all of Moon's senses told him that something had gone terribly wrong. His tongue could taste masonry dust above the soot and salt of the London air, and his ears could hear the whistling of falling objects, striking against the stonework as they raced to the ground. He winced as he heard something heavy hit the cobblestones fifty yards away from where he stood.

It sounded like a side of beef hitting the butcher's slab.

He ran, desperate to prove wrong what his ears had already told him to be true.

When Jago Moon kneeled beside the body he was grateful that he was a blind man. He knew it was Mother Shepherd – he recognized the smell of Sunlight soap and the rose water she always dabbed on her wrists. He placed his hand on hers and felt the warm stickiness of blood. And the faintest fluttering of a pulse.

"Mother Shepherd," he began, "I—"

She silenced him with a shaking finger pressed to his lips. "I don't have much time left in this world," she murmured. "I need you to make me a promise."

"Name it."

"Find Ben, no matter what it takes," she hissed urgently. "Ben was with me and we...argued. It was *my* fault, Jago, you must understand, *my fault*, not Ben's...

I...I failed him. I should have protected him from the Coin... I asked too much of him, too soon..." She broke off then, the effort of speaking taking its toll.

"Does Ben know where the last Judas Coin is?"

"It's been in his pocket the whole time."

Jago Moon was staggered. He couldn't imagine how much strength it must have taken to carry such a burden in secret.

"I tried to make him give me the Coin," Mother Shepherd explained. "I only wanted to help him but I ended up hurting him instead... Ben must be told that I don't blame him for what's happened, it was my fault, all of it... Find him, save him, Jago... Tell Ben that he is forgiven, that I love..."

And then she was gone. The brightest light in all of London, extinguished, dead in the dust of St Paul's.

The rope was ten feet short of the ground and Ben fell the last drop, the pain shooting up through his ankles. He didn't care about himself though. He spun around, looking for Mother Shepherd through the murk of the fog.

He saw the form of Jago Moon, hunched over a shape on the pavement.

He heard the old man's deep sobs.

As he watched, Jago Moon jerked his head up and Ben could feel the intensity of those blind eyes, even through the suffocating mist.

"Ben!" Moon shouted.

Ben ran.

CHAPTER 21

WAR!

Sweet sat upon the great golden throne in the sanctuary of the Under while the motley ranks of the Legion stood silently before him, waiting on his every word. They were not as well trained as the army, but what they lacked in ability they made up for in enthusiasm.

The sanctuary never failed to impress, Sweet thought. Although they were deep beneath the London clay, the vaulted ceiling rose high above their heads, held aloft by vast stone columns carved with the faces of beasts and men, their muscular arms arcing forward and meeting in the middle. In wrought-iron sconces and niches carved into the walls, a thousand candles burned with golden light; but there were not enough candles in the world to defeat the inky gloom of the sanctuary. It was a place where darkness was celebrated and shadows ruled. Sweet couldn't help but wonder how this throne would compare to the one in Buckingham Palace. *Not long now*, he reminded himself. Not long.

Mr. Sweet rose to his feet and every Legionnaire, every man, woman, boy and girl in their number, slapped their left fist against their breast. In the eaves above, roosting at the tops of the pillars, Feathered Men squawked their approval.

"Today is a glorious day for the Legion!" Mr. Sweet declared, his deep voice echoing into every corner. "Today marks our last day as an army in hiding!"

The crowd cheered.

"We have brought this city to its knees. The Government is ours!" *Mine, actually.* "We have the Watchers on the run."

The Legionnaires roared their approval.

"And now we will finish them!"

With that he signalled to a group of bare-chested Legionnaires standing beside an enormous crank, which operated a massive chain ascending into the blackest recess of the roof. The crowd watched in anticipation as the men took their places, bent low and began to heave against the wheel, like oxen grinding corn. It was agonizing at first and progress was slow. But then the cogs began to turn, taking up the slack in the chain, and gradually, notch by notch, a series of shutters began to open along the length of the sanctuary ceiling. With screams and shrieks the Feathered Men fell into a frenzy of excitement, sensing that their freedom was at hand.

"The ancient gates are being opened wide," said Sweet, his voice rising above the screeching of the winged monsters, the astonished murmurs of the crowd and the groans of the stone panels as they creaked slowly aside to reveal the open mouths of tunnels leading to the surface. "Today we see the birth of a new Legion, a stronger Legion." The crowd was in raptures as Mr. Sweet spoke. "This day I unleash the Feathered Men and let all of London quake!"

The Feathered Men began a cacophony of singing in their foul language, and like a flock of birds they acted as one, wheeling and turning around the roof of the sanctuary. Mr. Sweet watched the terrible cloud, and felt the downbeat of their wings, so vigorous that the candles began to gutter and die. Then, on some unseen command, the fallen angels flew into the waiting tunnels and swarmed away towards an unsuspecting London.

Mr. Sweet's ambition soared with them. In two short

days it would be the Feast of Ravens, the night when the powers of darkness were at their highest.

Who can stop me now? he wondered as he watched the last of the Feathered Men depart.

Lucy Lambert saw them first. She forced down the sickening fist of panic that rose inside her as she began to count the terrifying forms.

One. Two. Three.

Five.

Ten.

A whole squadron of Feathered Men had emerged from beneath the blanket of fog and was heading straight towards them, the mist eddying with the beating of their wings.

Lucy was standing guard on the roof of St Bart's and one look at the shivering, wounded bodies stretched out behind her was enough to convince her that there was no way these people were well enough to make an escape over the rooftops. She ran to the warning bell and struck it with a hammer. Its solemn toll rang out, deep and full of danger.

"To arms!" Lucy shouted. "Watchers to arms!"

The Feathered Men were still far away, but they were

closing in with every second. Flying in close formation and with one fixed intent: death.

Adrenaline surged through Lucy's veins as she ran to the defence post that was mounted on the corner of the rooftop in anticipation of an attack like this. She dragged the tarpaulin off, revealing the mounted harpoon gun beneath, its three metal support legs bolted to the roof, its bucket seat waiting for her. Lucy hesitated. She had trained for this, but she knew that there was going to be a world of difference between shooting at targets and trying to hit Feathered Men for real.

Ghost joined her and for a moment his brown eyes fixed on hers.

"I know," she said, grateful for his silent support. "We can do this."

Ghost grinned and took up his position on the crank handle while Lucy settled herself into the low-slung gunner's seat, leaning back and looking down the length of the barrel, getting her eye used to the sight. It was an impressive piece of equipment, fashioned from brass and steel. It was her job to aim and fire when the enemy was squarely in her sights. Ghost had a more physically demanding role, well suited to his impressive muscles. It was his task to turn the crank handle, spinning the weapon to the left or right in accordance with Lucy's instructions: that way they could aim the gun in any direction and track their enemy across the sky.

Behind them the rooftop was a flurry of movement, the hours of practising emergency drills paying off. The younger Watchers were gathering the refugees together and doing what they could to shelter them beneath heavy layers of canvas and tarp. Lucy spotted Molly Marbank helping an old lady under cover.

Other Watchers were getting ready to take their stand. Jonas Kingdom was a natural leader and she could hear his voice barking out, getting snipers into the best positions, their crossbows aimed on the oncoming foes. No padded heads on the crossbow bolts this time, Lucy noted grimly.

She had always understood that the Watchers were at war with the Legion, but today it became a reality. They had always been countering the Legion's plans in secret, foiling their schemes, generally spoiling their day. Now that had changed. No more hiding. This was open war.

As Lucy was thinking this, Josiah rushed past her and launched himself into the sky, diving like a hawk with his curved sword drawn and ready. Lucy knew that the sword's name was *Peace*. She also knew how much it hurt Josiah when he had to use it. Although they were hateful and had rejected everything that was good, the Feathered

Men were still Josiah's own kind: he would weep as he plunged his sword into their black and corrupted hearts.

"Brace yourself," hissed Lucy to Ghost as the Feathered Men drew nearer, "here comes the first wave."

As she watched, three of the creatures peeled off from the main formation and began to swoop down towards them. Lucy tracked the first one down the gleaming line of the harpoon gun.

"Incoming!" Lucy shouted. "Bearing at one o'clock!" In response Ghost furiously cranked the handles so that Lucy could keep the Feathered Man in her sights.

The fallen angel appeared in the cross hairs of the harpoon. Taking a deep breath, she pulled the trigger.

They both watched as the harpoon was released and spun through the air towards the Feathered Man, a thin guide rope snaking out behind it. Lucy found her knuckles going white as she gripped the handle of the massive gun, willing the missile to fly true. She saw the look of horror on the monster's face as it finally saw the spear that was heading its way.

Then it was her turn to be shocked as the Feathered Man weaved in the air, bending at the waist so that the harpoon missed him by an inch.

Enraged, the Feathered Man now looked back at Lucy through those same cross hairs and began to fly straight for her.

"Reload!" she shouted.

Ghost reached for a new harpoon, but his fingers were slick with sweat and he wasted precious seconds dropping it and picking it up again. Together they ratcheted back the spring-loaded mechanism and slid the fresh bolt down the barrel into the firing position.

By the time Lucy was back in the seat the Feathered Man was almost upon them.

"Three o'clock," she screamed and Ghost spun the gun round until she was face-to-face with the enemy.

Even at the battle of Tower Bridge, Lucy had never been this close to one of the fallen angels before. Part of her had always struggled to believe that these once beautiful creatures didn't still retain an ounce of goodness somewhere deep inside. But now that she looked one of the beasts in the eye, and saw in those dark mirrors nothing but hatred, she could pull the trigger with a clean conscience. If she didn't stop this *thing*, then it wouldn't hesitate to tear her to pieces.

The bolt struck the Feathered Man square in the chest, the tip emerging from its back with a spurt of dark blood.

Lucy watched as it fell, spinning to its death, its wings collapsed like broken sails.

"Reload," she said calmly. "Two more coming in. Twelve o'clock."

CHAPTER 22

THE WALKING WOUNDED

Ben ran until his legs gave out. His muscles burned and he lost all control of his limbs, wobbling like a calf before stumbling face down onto the ground.

When Mother Shepherd fell, Ben felt something snap inside of him. He almost heard it crack, as if it were a physical thing. Did hearts really break like they said so in stories? he wondered. His felt as if his had.

Mother Shepherd loved him; that was the truth. In the time that they had been together, that frail but incredible old woman had shown him the tenderness and mother-love that his heart had always yearned for.

And now he had killed her. He heard the accusation

in Moon's cries as he fled the scene in shame.

His own voice condemned him too. *That's two mothers you've sent to the grave.*

Ben lay in the gutter. The cobbles were wet and the dampness was soaking into his clothes. He would have stayed there if a pair of feet hadn't walked into his line of vision. Even then he wouldn't have moved if it had been any old pair of boots, even Constable Wilde's, all polished and shiny from kicking Old Gravel Lane boys up the backside. But these weren't any old boots. They weren't really even feet.

Ben was staring at the talons of a Feathered Man.

Still shaky, Ben hauled himself upright again. The filthy creature circled him, its beak opening and closing slowly, revealing its thin black tongue. Its huge wings were spread wide, closing him in on two sides. It made an angry hiss and then launched itself at him, slashing at his face with its claws.

"So, you want to cut up rusty, eh?" Ben muttered, as he dodged and unhooked the collapsible quarterstaff from his belt, extending it to its full five-foot length. "That suits me fine, mate," he said, as he unleashed a furious attack.

The Feathered Man was taken aback by the aggression of Ben's assault, and raised its long bony arms to shield its head from the strikes of the quarterstaff. Ben took all his anger, pain and guilt and channelled them into the movement of his weapon.

Jago Moon had trained him well, Ben realized, as he landed blow after blow on the creature. Seeing a gap in its defences, Ben switched tactics and lunged his staff straight into the Feathered Man's stomach. With a certain satisfaction, Ben saw its muscles contract with the force of his blow and heard a winded gasp emerge from the fallen angel's throat.

But the Feathered Man was not beaten yet.

It extended its huge wings to their full expanse and lifted itself into the air so that it was beyond the reach of Ben's swinging staff. Then it hovered, its legs drawn up, the talons of its feet bared towards Ben, like a kestrel waiting to snatch a rabbit.

Ben feinted to the right and the creature matched his move. He made for the left and it followed him again. And when the fallen angel went in for the kill it dropped on him with incredible speed. Ben tried to use his quarterstaff to knock those dreadful talons away but he was just too slow. The Feathered Man locked its feet tight around Ben's throat and then began to drag him up into the sky, hissing in triumph.

Ben was convinced that his head was going to become detached from his body. Frantically he tried to get his own fingers around the creature's elongated toes and prise them away from his throat before his windpipe burst, but the Feathered Man squeezed all the harder until the blood pounded in Ben's ears.

With a sense of resignation Ben stopped struggling. He couldn't budge those savage talons and he couldn't escape the final image of Mother Shepherd's face. Wouldn't it be better for the Watchers if he let the Legion kill him now and have done with it?

The veins at his temples stood proud as the pressure around his throat increased. His lungs were a furnace. His vision began to swim… The flow of oxygen ceased to Ben's brain and he sensed his body starting to shut down as the Feathered Man's claws continued to squeeze the life out of him.

A face swam into his mind: his father, Jonas Kingdom.

Then Jago Moon. The Weeping Man.

Lucy Lambert…

Nathaniel!

Ben opened his eyes in time to see the lamp post rushing towards him. He knew that he would only get one chance. He loosened his shoulder pack so that the stout leather strap was hanging free, like a noose. He hoped and prayed that the Feathered Man would fly close enough for this to work. When he had positioned the strap as best he could, Ben clung to the fallen angel's ankles with all his might, and braced himself for the moment of impact.

Luck, or perhaps a higher power, was on Ben's side, and as his bag snagged on the lamp post, Ben was yanked backwards with a terrible jolt. Amazingly, the strap didn't rip free from the pack as Ben had feared, and instead it yanked the Feathered Man to a halt in mid-flight. Ben was grateful that he had been holding tight to the Feathered Man's ankles, as that had probably saved his neck from being snapped. It also meant that, as the stunned creature loosened its grip, Ben kept a firm hold, and as he fell, suspended from the top of the lamp post by his backpack, he was able to swing the Feathered Man downwards in an arc, like a pendulum, until the creature's face hit the cast-iron upright.

Letting go of the fallen angel, Ben tugged his bag free and dropped down onto the cobbles.

Behind him he could hear the Feathered Man writhing in pain. Its face was a broken mess, the beak shattered. It gave a final dreadful screech and then, to Ben's relief, it died.

Ben felt no triumph, no joy.

He had been the cause of two deaths that day. One Legionnaire. One Watcher.

Ben turned up his collar and walked away into the mist, hoping to lose himself for ever.

The battle of St Bart's was over, for the moment. The Watchers had fought the Feathered Men off, although victory had come at a price. Several of the refugees were laid out beneath whatever blankets could be found. They were mostly elderly, their bodies not up to the demands of fighting, but some were young, and perhaps had been too brave for their own good.

The Watchers that remained were battered and bruised, exhausted but still standing. Jonas Kingdom wore a bandage round his head where a Feathered Man had caught him with a glancing blow. Lucy had felt the rake of claws down her own arm, but she refused to make a fuss, binding it herself with her scarf, never abandoning her post on the harpoon gun.

It was Josiah, the Weeping Man, who had won the day for them. They all knew that without his great skill with the sword there would have been twice as many casualties. Lucy had seen him battling with Feathered Men in the sky above her head, weeping as they left him no choice but to plunge his sword into their hearts.

There was no rejoicing or celebration to mark the end

of fighting, but a sense of quiet contemplation settled on them all as they tended to the wounded. They had survived, they were alive; that was a blessing, at least.

When Jago Moon returned to the eyrie that peace was shattered.

A deep and profound shock fell upon them all as they tried to make sense of the body that he was cradling tenderly in his arms. Then the tears began. Gently, Jago Moon lowered Mother Shepherd to the ground and sat silently at her side, his old fingers knitted with hers. Lucy crouched beside Mother Shepherd's beautiful face. One by one, the other Watchers came and stood around in silence, their heads bowed, their eyes red.

Mother Shepherd looked so serene, Lucy thought. She had always carried light within her and even in death her face shone. Jago Moon refused to speak, or perhaps wasn't able to say what had happened, his jaws clenched tight in grief. But within moments, roof-runners were sent out to pass on the terrible news to every Watcher camp across the city. First one church bell began to ring mournfully, then another, and another, until across the rooftops of London all of the Watchers were united in their grief.

After a few minutes the tolling stopped; a final solemn note rolled out across the fog. It was the darkest day that

Lucy had known since her father and brother had been taken from her. Death, in all its misery, had found her again.

The emptiness they all felt was vast and aching, and yet Mother Shepherd would want them to continue, Lucy knew that. There wasn't time for mourning. The Feathered Men had found their makeshift base at St Bart's and could return at any moment. So for now they had to up sticks and move again. The Watchers worked together, and as quickly as they were able, they decamped to the roof of Tranter's Temperance Hotel on Bridgewater Square. It was really no distance from the hospital at all, although with their army of walking wounded, it may as well have been a hundred miles away. But the main advantage Tranter's had was that the roof was just below the level of the mist and so at least it made them harder to spot.

Jonas Kingdom and his team were making excellent progress with the Liberator under the most extreme circumstances, but there was a fear at the back of Lucy's mind that it might all be just too late. She was also aware that, as tired as they were, they wouldn't be able to rest at Tranter's for long. The Watchers would have to keep moving if they were to have any chance of staying one step ahead of the Legion now.

Jago Moon drew her to one side, where Josiah was

waiting patiently. She looked at their faces and braced herself.

"Mother Shepherd spoke to me, before…" Moon's voice cracked. "…before it was all over. Ben was with her at St Paul's and they argued. There was an accident and… well, you know the rest… She kept insisting that it was *her* fault, that she had allowed Ben to carry more responsibility than he was able to bear."

Lucy tried to piece the picture together in her mind, horrified at the image she created. "What was the fight about?"

"The Coin," said Josiah. "Ben is carrying the last of the Thirty."

The Coin! Lucy was shocked. Two emotions clashed inside her. Pity: she couldn't imagine how much torment Ben must have felt carrying that cursed thing around the whole time. And anger: how could he have been so stupid? Risking his life…risking *all* their lives…and now Mother Shepherd was gone.

"So what next?" she said.

"We find him," said Moon. "We need Ben, now more than ever."

CHAPTER 23

BACK FROM THE DEAD

Although the fog still made blind men of them all, somehow Ben had managed to find his way back to Old Gravel Lane. He wondered if perhaps there would be some comfort for him here, back where he had belonged before he found himself in the middle of a war. This was the street where his family had lived; it was on these cobbles that he had larked around with the other street urchins, throwing jacks and picking pockets; getting his ears boxed. Grand times for the most part – except for the grinding poverty and the constant hunger that gnawed in his belly, obviously.

It all seemed a lifetime ago. Coming back now, Ben felt like a stranger.

He was all but alone on the street, a solitary shadow stumbling through the fog. Occasionally he saw the outline of another wanderer in the white, but they always kept their distance, moving away as quickly as possible. Probably weary of being accosted, Ben thought; there was no safety in London any more. Everyone with any sense had shut, locked and barred their door. The shops were boarded up. All the shutters were down. Planks had been hammered hastily over windows and signs painted to deter looters: **No valuables inside.** Or the rather more direct: **An Englishman's home is his castle and I shall defend it!**

Welcome home, Benny boy. Ain't life grand?

The Lane had always been full of noise and bustle, and more than anything it was the strange stillness which unnerved Ben now. The few sounds that did reach out through the mist brought no reassurance: muttering behind closed doors; a woman mumbling incoherently; a cat hissing at some unseen foe; a bottle rolling on the cobblestones; a child calling for a mother who wasn't coming home.

It was like a ghost town, he thought. Even the docks were silent, the cargo ships grounded by the uncanny fog. He brought his face up close to the window of a sailors' outfitters. Normally it would have been full of bright blue and red flannel shirts, hammocks, nor'westers, canvas trousers, rough pilot coats, and ship's biscuits "guaranteed to keep in any climate", but the window had been smashed and the contents were all long gone. Ben studied himself in a broken shard of glass still clinging to the frame. It was the first time he had seen his reflection since the fog had fallen and he was shocked by what he saw.

He looked older, for one thing, and tired too. He had lost some weight in his cheeks, so that the face that stared back at him was squarer than the one he remembered, beginning to leave childhood behind.

So this was the face of the boy who killed Mother Shepherd.

There could be no going back, not after what he had done. Perhaps once he had dreamed that he truly could be the Hand of Heaven, but that path was closed now.

So where did that leave him?

On my own and on the run again, he supposed. *The story of my life.*

A shadow moved across the window and a hot breath on the back of his neck warned Ben that he was wrong on one count – he wasn't alone.

He spun, fists raised, ready for a fight. When he saw who it was, Ben put his hands down but kept his guard up.

It was a girl, with cropped hair that stood up at odd

angles. A girl with green leather gloves, a velvet jacket and emerald eyes which flashed at him through the gloom.

"Hello, Benjamin," Ruby purred. "Where did you get that tatty old hat?"

"I thought you were dead, Ruby."

"I make it a rule never to judge by appearances," she replied.

"Why are you here, Ruby?" Ben said angrily. He didn't want to be near anybody. People got hurt when he was around.

"You know I like to keep an eye out for you, Ben," she said. "You always seem to be getting yourself into scrapes."

"Nothing I can't handle."

"Really?" She arched an eyebrow.

"I've left the Watchers, that's all," he said. The sound of those words spoken out loud was shocking to his ears.

"I'm not surprised," said Ruby.

"Really? Why?"

"Because I know you better than you know yourself, Ben Kingdom." She said it with a wink and Ben felt the pull of her emerald eyes.

"Go on then," he challenged, his voice softening. "Prove it."

Ruby paused. "You've got the gift of the gab and you think you look the business. When you were younger you dreamed of adventure but now you're in the middle of one, you're not so sure. You always wondered if there was something special about you, but you're afraid of the responsibility of leadership because in your heart you don't want to let anyone down."

"Anything else?"

"You like pork pies."

"Everyone likes pork pies."

"Not as much as you, they don't," Ruby continued. "Was I close?"

"Nah," said Ben. "Nowhere near. Except for the bit about pies."

Except on every point.

"What makes you think you're an expert on me anyway?" said Ben.

"Because I like you," Ruby answered. "Because I listen to the things that you say when we're together."

Ben hesitated. He had been down this path before and look where that had got him.

And yet here was someone who knew about him and still wanted to be his friend. There couldn't be too many of those left in London. Ben felt himself slipping back into his old ways; pretending that nothing bothered him, acting as Jack the Lad to make up for the ache of guilt and fear and shame inside.

Ruby smiled. "I think we make a good team, Ben. Won't you join me?"

Just then, an idea occurred to Ben. Ruby could get him into the Under. Ruby could lead him to Nathaniel. Ben *still* might be able to rescue his brother. He smiled in return

Unexpectedly, Ruby flung her arms around Ben's neck. He didn't understand what she was doing until she stepped away and he felt the folds of a silk scarf around his neck.

"Why did you do that?" said Ben.

Ruby shrugged. "I can't have you going around looking like a tramp, can I?"

It was a nice scarf, Ben had to admit, as he tucked it inside his jacket and turned up his collar.

"How do I look?" he asked.

Ruby smiled. "You'll do."

"Lead on then, Miss Johnson," said Ben, putting on his brave act. *Same old, same old,* he thought, as he followed her through the fog.

Ben couldn't imagine how his life would ever move on from that morning. Mother Shepherd had told him how powerful forgiveness was, and yet he doubted that he would ever be able to forgive himself. Josiah had taught

Ben that life was all about choices, but more than that, the angel had explained that it was how a person reacts *after* they have made a bad choice that makes the difference between a life of purpose and a life wasted. But really, what choice did he have now? Ben asked himself. Mother Shepherd was dead because of him. What was he supposed to do? Go to the Watchers and say, "Sorry I killed your great leader, please forgive me... What's for tea?"

And yet the possibility of being reunited with Nathaniel kept a spark of hope glowing inside him. Maybe they could save each other?

Ruby lifted a manhole cover to reveal a ladder. Silently Ben followed her down the rungs, letting the darkness of the tunnel swallow him completely.

Ruby had promised him that he could lay low in the Under. She said that he could stay there for a while and no one need know. Unfortunately they hadn't gone ten yards when he was spotted. The man obviously recognized him and immediately scurried off back the way he'd come. After that, the news of Ben's return seemed to spread like wildfire. No matter which tunnel Ruby took, it felt as if they were expected. Faces peered out at them from behind doors, people stopped and gawped. First in ones and twos, then in groups. Standing. Staring.

And then the murmuring started.

It's him!

He's the one!

That's Ben Kingdom!

Whichever way they turned, they couldn't escape the strange whispering mob. Ben and Ruby exchanged an anxious glance.

Picking up their pace, they pelted away together along the corridor, trying to put some distance between themselves and the crowds. Ben soon began to recognize the tunnels and had to push down a sense of dread. Ruby was taking him back to where it had all begun.

He would rather be anywhere else and yet Ben had no choice but to keep running.

I'll find you, Nathaniel. And then we can both get the hell out of here.

"Hello, lads, did you miss me?" Ben stood in the barracks' doorway and did his best to sound casual, as if he had nipped out for a bag of chestnuts and was late getting back. He didn't want to give these dangerous boys even a hint of the vulnerability he felt inside. However, judging by the way they were all looking at him, Ben could tell they weren't having any of it.

There was unfinished business between them, after all.

Such as Ben abandoning the Legion the last time he had been here and bringing down a length of tunnel on their heads as a leaving present. Plus there'd been that little scuffle just last night.

Hans Schulman regarded him coldly, his face more world-weary than Ben had ever seen it. Alexander Valentine didn't appear to have moved since Ben had left months ago; he was still lying on his bunk. He was one step nearer the grave, Ben guessed, judging by the pale blue tint of his lips and the red bubbles he blew each time he coughed. Jimmy Dips was there, nursing his resentment. Then there was Munro, the hunchback, who always reminded Ben of a mistreated animal: nervous and subservient but waiting for his chance to bite back. Beside him was Buster, his three-legged bulldog, who took this opportunity to welcome Ben by hopping closer and peeing on his foot.

John Bedlam was there too, the little yob, still yearning for a fight. And Mickelwhite, obviously ready to pick things up where they'd left off.

Ben felt their eyes drilling into him.

"We saw you," said Mickelwhite, his words laden with meaning.

"You saw me?" Ben wasn't following.

"We saw you," Mickelwhite repeated. His lips formed a twisted smile. "This morning."

This morning.

Bedlam was grinning too, an ugly sneer.

They saw me, this morning. Ben's heart filled with dread.

"On St Paul's," Mickelwhite continued, milking every moment, "with the Hag."

Ben wanted to say something, to deny it, but his tongue was as dry as old leather in his mouth. *They know*, he thought with despair. *They know the secret that I would have given my soul to keep hidden.*

"We saw it all, through our telescopes," said Mickelwhite, his cruel grin growing wider. "We don't stay in the Under *all* the time, you know. We go up onto the high places as well, to watch the Watchers." His tongue touched the tips of his teeth, savouring the words. "We saw the mighty anger rising up inside you, we saw the violence erupt. We saw your fist smashing the stonework – that withered old witch was terrified... You were magnificent!"

"We saw the whole thing," Bedlam chimed in, "brilliant, it was. You were shouting in her face and you went so red we thought you were going to bust a blood vessel."

"And then you killed her," Mickelwhite finished.

Ben examined the faces around him. He'd thought that they had been glaring at him when he arrived, but now he realized that he had read their emotions all wrong.

206

They were staring at him with admiration – and maybe a tinge of fear.

Mickelwhite began to clap and the others followed until Ben's ears were echoing with their applause. They gathered round him and embraced him like a brother, like a hero.

"So you were pretending all along," said Bedlam. "You made us believe that you had gone over to the Watchers, but it was a lie!"

Ben felt his heart sink down into his boots.

Perhaps it was, he thought.

Perhaps this gutter is where I belong?

CHAPTER 24

HERO OF THE LEGION

Ben could think of nothing to say as Mickelwhite and his brigade bundled him through the corridors of the Under, cheering and telling everyone they met about Ben's act of murder.

"He killed 'er!" Bedlam yelled at the top of his voice. "The Hag is dead and Ben Kingdom done it!"

The triumphant chant was taken up, echoing down the tunnels. "Kingdom! Kingdom! Kingdom!"

It was a mistake! Ben wanted to shout. *I never meant to hurt her.* And yet he couldn't make the words form on his tongue. Only Ruby Johnson didn't seem to share the Legion's excitement. When Ben stole a glance in her direction, there was a sense of deadness in her eyes too, as if she, like him, was removed from what was going on around her. But she wouldn't return his gaze and when his fingers sought the reassurance of her grasp she pulled away. Ben couldn't say he blamed her.

It was impossible for Ben to guess how long that journey took. The whole time he had the sense that he was trapped in a nightmare. He wanted to scream but his lips were sealed; he wanted to act but he was powerless. At some point, Mickelwhite and the others hoisted Ben up onto their shoulders and they carried him like some sort of champion, only setting his feet back on the ground when they were in Carter's rooms beneath the British Museum.

Professor Carter rose from his desk, came over to Ben…and embraced him, as warmly as Mother Shepherd once had. There was no mention of the battle they had fought for possession of the missing Coin. Or of the uncomfortable fact that Ben hadn't seen Carter's claw since it had slit his father's throat. Mother Shepherd's death, it would seem, had wiped the slate clean.

Claw Carter welcomed him like a hero.

"Ben, my boy!" said Carter, beaming. "I always knew you belonged with me."

It was meant as a compliment, Ben supposed, yet Carter had given voice to his deepest fear…

So I really am going to be the Hand of Hell, after all.

It was the darkest thought Ben had ever known.

"You have nothing to be ashamed of, Ben, I hope you realize that."

Claw Carter had been talking with Ben like that for over an hour. Saying all the things that Ben's troubled heart so desperately needed to hear.

It had been obvious to Carter that Ben was overwhelmed with emotion and he had quickly ushered all the others away until the two of them were alone in the privacy of his room. For his part, Ben had hardly breathed a word. He let his eyes wander over the professor's collection of treasures: skulls of every shape and size, their empty sockets gazing back at him.

He looked everywhere except at Carter, but his ears took in everything the man said.

"You can't blame a dog for barking, Ben. You might not like the noise it makes, but dogs bark; it's their nature and they have no control over it. You are the Hand of Hell, Benjamin, you have to stop fighting that fact and just accept it. You *will* destroy the Watchers, that's *your* nature, and you are wrong to resist following it. I hope," said Carter, resting his good hand on Ben's shoulder, "that you will allow me the honour of being your guide. You must embrace your destiny, Ben; take pleasure in the power you wield."

Ben thought for a moment. "And if I do that, you'll take me to Nathaniel? Release him?"

"Your brother isn't *my* prisoner, Ben, but, of course, that will be our very first aim…providing you join with me."

Ben still hesitated, not ready to utter the words aloud. "But…" he began.

"Go on," Carter urged gently. "I've sat in your position, I've wrestled with the same questions you are battling now."

"But if I am…"

"The Hand of Hell…" Carter filled in the gaps.

"If I am…*that*…doesn't that make me evil?"

Carter laughed out loud. "Who says?"

Well, thought Ben, *Cowpat Cowper, for one. And Pa, and Nathaniel, and Mr. Moon, and Lucy Lambert… And me.*

"Just about everyone," Ben replied.

"Everyone is wrong," said Carter. "There is no such thing as good or evil."

"Of course there is," Ben spluttered.

Carter shook his head. "Good and evil, right and wrong, are all merely man-made concepts. Artificial rules invented to control the masses."

Ben couldn't agree. What Carter was saying went against everything he had ever understood about the world. "That's not true," he said.

"Give me an example then, Ben," said Carter. "Tell me something which you think is evil."

"Killing," Ben replied instantly. "It's wrong to kill."

"Is it?" said Carter. "What about if you are defending yourself, if you are fighting for your own life?"

"Well, in that case, no, but—"

"Give me another example then."

"Stealing."

"If you are starving? Are you telling me that it's evil to steal bread if you have nothing to eat?"

"No," Ben conceded again.

"So killing and stealing aren't always wrong, are they?" Carter sounded very persuasive.

"Not if you put it like that."

"And you must put it like that too, Ben. Forget all about good and evil. Life is about survival, and the sooner you start seeing it like that, the sooner you will be free to live exactly the way you want to. Without guilt, without remorse, and without any petty rules to hold you back. Like me. "

Ben's head was spinning. He could see the logic in Carter's argument and yet it still felt twisted.

"Do we consider lions to be evil when they kill gazelles? Do we call a raven a thief when it takes food to feed itself? No, we call this the survival of the fittest. Why should different rules apply to us?"

"Because we aren't animals, Professor Carter."

"Aren't we? What makes us so special?" He swung his claw towards his shelves of bones. "Strip away our flesh and you'll find we are all the same on the inside. Kill or be killed is the only law which applies to us all."

"So if what we call 'good' or 'evil' just depends which side we're looking from, then how come the Watchers have got an angel fighting with them?"

"So have the Legion," Carter retorted. "Or have you forgotten the Feathered Men?"

Ben thought of their angry unblinking eyes, their snapping beaks, their fetid breath, the talons that he had seen rip a man in two.

"Oh," said Carter, reading the expression on Ben's face, "I see. Just because the Weeping Man is more handsome and eloquent, that makes him better, does it? His wings are white are so that means he must be the good guy?"

"At least his wings aren't stained with blood."

"Aren't they? I seem to remember him being rather handy with that sword of his. The Watchers really have got their claws deeply into you, haven't they?" Carter

213

added with a sudden flash of anger. "I have a very easy relationship with their precious Uncreated One. He hates me and I hate Him." Slowly, Claw Carter reached over to his desk and opened a drawer. "Let me show you why."

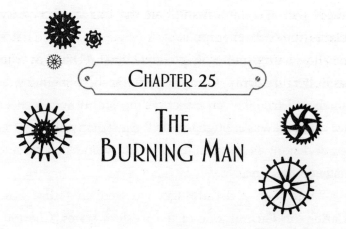

CHAPTER 25

THE
BURNING MAN

The woman in the photograph was incredibly beautiful, Ben thought. What he liked best about her was her smile. Ben could imagine her bursting into laughter the second the photograph had been taken, filling the room with her joy.

"She's lovely," said Ben.

"Thank you," said Carter softly, "I think so. That's why I married her. Her name is Charlotte...*was* Charlotte, I should say. She's dead now." Ben saw the tears that welled in Carter's eyes and felt a sudden compassion. Ben knew all too well what it felt like to miss the most important woman in your world. He thought of his mother every single day and the echoing hole that her death had left inside him had never healed.

"It was a mosquito," Carter explained. "That was what stole her life away. Can you imagine it? Something as small and trivial as an insect resting on my wife's cheek for a second was enough to ruin the rest of my life." Carter grew distant as he continued his story and Ben sat and listened in silence.

"More than a decade ago, we were in India," said Carter, "in Gujarat, one of the western states. Charlotte and I were embarking on an expedition together. I had a young man's dream of trekking up the Indus Valley and finding the lost golden calf of Harappa. We were going to be rich!" He gave a hollow laugh. "The risk of malaria was well-documented but I was a seasoned explorer and thought that mosquito nets would be enough to protect us. I was wrong, Ben. One tiny malaria-ridden fly got through Charlotte's net while she was sleeping and killed her.

"She didn't die instantly, of course. First she had to endure a week of shaking, misery and sweat while the disease had its way with her. I could do nothing except watch helplessly and pray for her recovery. But my prayers went unanswered. One pinprick from the mosquito, Ben, and my wife was gone...and the baby she carried inside her was lost to me before it even took its first breath."

A tear rolled down Carter's lined and rutted cheek and he did nothing to hide it. "I buried my wife and unborn child at the Sun Temple at Modhera and then I walked away. I took nothing with me – no supplies, no maps, not even a water flask. My only possession was my anger and it drove me blindly onwards. I think that in my grief I went slightly mad, Ben. I kept walking north until I came to the Thar Desert, the great plain of sands in Rajasthan, which the locals called the *Lavansagara*, the ocean of salt. I had no plans to ever return.

"The heat was blistering. I made no effort to stop it sucking the last of the moisture from my body, but even the sun didn't burn as fiercely as my rage. I was delirious by that stage, probably only an hour or two from death by dehydration. When I saw the figure walking towards me over the dunes, I thought that he was a mirage at first, the last imaginations of my fevered brain.

"He had the physique of a warrior, Ben, as if he was a Greek statue come to life. His pace was unhurried and he carried himself with the arrogance of a king. I knew how my own skin was suffering in the blazing heat, my lips were cracked and bleeding, but this man... He was on fire."

Ben gasped.

"I didn't know whether I could trust my own eyes," Carter said. "I had seen fakirs walking on hot coals without wincing, but this was entirely different. I remember that I stood there, mesmerized, as fire caressed his entire body but apparently left him unharmed. It was beautiful, Ben. I watched the flames dance on his muscled arms and blossom around his head like a halo. They even flickered along the length of the enormous wings that sprouted from his shoulders. You can see why I thought I was hallucinating.

"The angel spoke to me, Ben. He knew my name and said that my anger had called out to him across the miles. I was furious! If this being had been sent down to comfort me, then I didn't want to hear anything it had to say!"

Carter paused to compose himself. Even though the story was more than a decade old, it was clear to Ben that the professor's wounds were still raw.

"Then the Burning Man smiled at me. I saw the perfect pointed teeth that filled his mouth like a piranha's and I knew that wherever he came from, it wasn't Heaven. We talked for hours in that desert. And all the while I could see vultures circling above our heads, waiting for the moment that I became another carcass for them to dine on.

As my life ebbed away, the Burning Man shared his secrets with me. He told me that he knew what it was like to be angry with the Uncreated One, because *he* was the angriest of all.

"'An eye for an eye', Ben, have you heard that expression? That was what the Burning Man was offering me: revenge on the Uncreated One who had ignored my cries." Small flecks of spit escaped Carter's lips as he grew more animated. "The Burning Man told me of an ancient alliance between fallen angels and man…"

"The Legion," said Ben.

"Exactly," said Carter, "the most diverse army in the world, whose stories are as varied as the grains of sand in that desert. But we all share one thing in common, Ben, a tie that binds us together – our shared desire to overthrow the Uncreated One."

Claw Carter looked straight at Ben and for the first time Ben could see the vulnerability that lurked behind the man's steel-grey eyes.

"I was on the verge of death when the Burning Man gave a signal and the vultures began to drop. But as they flew closer I saw that they weren't vultures at all; they were men with the wings and heads of eagles… I don't know how long the Feathered Men tended to me in that desert, but I know that when I returned to civilization and the company of men, I was ready to pledge my life to the Legion.

"I loved Charlotte," Carter said, "but the Uncreated One took her from me. So now I choose not to live by His rules. Your mother was stolen from you, wasn't she? You understand how I feel, don't you, Ben?"

"Yes," said Ben quietly. "I do."

CHAPTER 26

NO PRISONERS

Find Ben. That was the thought in all of their minds as the three Watchers groped their way through the rolling sea of vapour.

Jago Moon could feel the fog all around him. Its gossamer fingers clung to his skin like a spider's web. The mist quivered and trembled as he passed through it, as though it contained a life of its own. It did little to improve his mood.

Mother Shepherd is dead. The words rang continuously inside his head. Moon felt as if huge chunks of his own life had crumbled into dust along with her. He couldn't allow himself the luxury of mourning though; he had responsibilities, he reminded himself – there were others who still depended on him. Not least of whom was Ben Kingdom.

The streets were virtually deserted. Part of the explanation for this, Moon had no doubt, were the soldiers patrolling the city in an attempt to restore order. An uneasy quiet had fallen across the city, and the sense of fear was as suffocating as the fog.

He led Lucy and Ghost onwards through the eerie silence. Looking for one boy in London was like looking for a needle in a haystack, which was why Moon had called in a few favours.

I may be the ears of London, he thought to himself, *but eyes come in handy now and then too.*

Moon had his own network of contacts whom he could call upon in situations such as this. Men and women from all walks of life who kept their eyes open and their wits sharp. Some of them were fully fledged Watchers, others were merely sympathetic to the cause, but they were all well placed and well informed. There was Sherrinford Morley, the celebrated actor, who knew every coming and going in the West End, and Lady Persephone Peters, who kept Moon up to date with all the gossip from society circles. Then there were his associates who moved amongst far less exalted company: Harry Gore, the Sea Wolf, who controlled every villain in the London docks, and Vladimir Kiskov of the infamous Red Hands, a gang leader and conman, who went some way to cleansing his conscience by spying for the Watchers. And then he had other informers who swam in darker waters still...

Moon heard the soldiers first.

Above the soft leather squeaks made by the Watcher coats worn by Lucy and Ghost, he could make out the soft rhythmic chiming of medals on a broad chest and the unmistakable crunch of army-issue "ammunition boots", with their iron heel and toe plates and studded leather soles. Moon counted the footsteps; three soldiers were approaching them from behind. *Armed* soldiers, he realized, as he heard the deafening click of a Mark IV Martini-Henry rifle being cocked.

"*Halt!*" shouted one of the soldiers. "Who goes there?"

"Let me handle this," Moon hissed, pausing in his tracks and spreading his arms wide as he turned to face the soldiers. "There's no trouble here, sir," he called to them.

"Step forward where we can see you," the soldier barked.

"We're not looters," said Moon, keeping his tone very level so as not to cause undue alarm. "I'm only a blind man and these two kind souls are helping me find my way home..."

Two more rifles cocked. "This doesn't look good," Lucy whispered.

"You don't keep very good company, old man," said the soldier. "I can see from the uniforms that your young associates are anarchists… My orders are to shoot Watcher revolutionaries on sight. The only question I have left is whether I have to shoot you too, just to be on the safe side."

"Quick!" Jago Moon whispered out of the corner of his mouth. "You two head for the rooftops, I'll tidy up here."

Lucy tutted loudly in response; he could almost hear her eyebrows rising in indignation.

"Alright," Moon muttered, "forget I even suggested it."

Raising his voice again he addressed the soldiers, while his hand moved slowly towards his cane and the sword which lay hidden within.

"There's been some sort of mistake, sir," said Moon, "we don't mean any harm."

"We shoot anarchists," the officer replied. "Orders are orders."

"Think for yourself, man!" Moon snapped back, his fingers now resting on the handle of his hidden blade. "I'm blind, and my associates are children. How much of a threat do you think we are?"

"You can take your hand off that swordstick for starters!" the officer shouted. "I wasn't born yesterday." Moon could tell from the anxiety in the man's voice that they were probably less than five seconds away from bullets being fired.

Moon sensed Lucy and Ghost readying themselves for his signal. He would have been altogether happier if they were up against Legion scum, rather than these strung-out soldiers. Obediently, he let his cane clatter to the ground.

"The Watchers aren't troublemakers," Moon explained in measured tones as he lifted his hands gently upwards, as if in surrender. "We don't have any fight with you."

"That's not what Mr. Sweet says," the soldier retorted.

"Oh," said Moon, fiddling absently with his scarf. "We *do* have a fight with him."

Without warning, Moon flicked out with the weapon concealed beneath his scarf. The bolas was a length of twisted wire, weighted by a heavy ball at each end. One fist-like weight whipped the cord around the barrel of the rifle that was aimed at Moon's chest, allowing the old man to wrench the gun from the surprised soldier's grasp. Lucy and Ghost leaped into action alongside him. Moon heard Lucy take a dozen graceful running steps and then extend her quarterstaff. She planted it squarely in the ground and vaulted neatly up and over another soldier's head, before he could bring his rifle to bear on her. With one of her favourite moves, she flicked out a roundhouse kick which sent the startled man flying. Ghost, meanwhile, had taken a running leap and grabbed hold of the arm of a gas lamp. Then, like some gymnast in the circus, he swung himself by both arms and kicked the remaining soldier over; the man's rifle discharged into the sky as he staggered to the cobblestones.

"Now," said Lucy breathlessly, "we can *all* run."

CHAPTER 27

THE DARK LIBRARY

Ben walked beside Claw Carter. They were going to the Dark Library – the Legion's book repository, buried deep in the lowest levels of the Under.

"I have found something that will be of great interest to you, my boy," said Carter with an enthusiasm that Ben couldn't share. With every step Ben took down the cold stone stairs, he could feel his trepidation growing. Carter had told him that there was no such thing as evil – and Ben was certain that Carter himself believed that to be true – but Ben was not so sure. What he did know was that he had to play along with Carter for a while, at least. Carter was willing to be his ally and could be the only way he had of reaching Nathaniel. This was such a dangerous game and Ben knew that he couldn't put a foot wrong.

He hadn't forgotten the Coin lurking in his pocket either. Ben didn't dare touch it, though. Not so long ago, all he wanted to do was to hold it in his hand, but it scared the life out of him now. He was terrified that it would fill him with its evil again. He was equally afraid that the Legion might find it on him. Yet something told him to hang on to it for a while. It might still prove to be his final bargaining chip to save his brother from becoming the sacrifice at the Feast.

At the bottom of the stairs they were greeted by a Feathered Man, crouching on its haunches in the torchlight. It was an especially ugly specimen, Ben thought. Its feathers were a dirty black and its beak was criss-crossed with battle scars. It rose up to its full height as they approached and hissed furiously.

"Down!" ordered Carter, and the foul creature stepped aside.

Carter opened the door with a flourish. "All of the hidden wisdom of the world," he said, "at *our* disposal."

To Ben's eyes it looked more like a crypt than a library. There were bookshelves, true enough, probably half a mile or more of them in the low vaulted room. But Ben couldn't take his gaze from the tombs that lay alongside them.

"Fallen heroes of the Legion," Carter explained, as they went inside. "No church would ever offer a resting place for them." He smiled. "You and I might find ourselves down here one day."

"What a cheery thought," said Ben.

The roof was supported by ornate columns, typical of Legion craftsmanship. Ben studied the carving of a fat snake entwined around one pillar. It was incredibly detailed, he thought, as he reached out to touch its diamond-shaped head...only to snatch his hand away again when a black tongue flicked out to taste the air.

"The snakes keep the rats down," said Carter. "After all, the knowledge contained in this vault is irreplaceable."

"And if I get bitten and lose my arm, I can always get a false one like you."

Carter turned on him, but instead of the anger that Ben had expected to see on the professor's face, there was an expression of amusement. "Come and take a seat beside me," he said, ushering Ben over to a broad desk strewn with papers.

Ben picked his way carefully across the flagstones. There was never enough light in the Under, and as much as he hated rats, the idea of stepping on a snake didn't fill him with joy either. He sat down in the chair next to Carter and drew his legs right up underneath him, just to be on the safe side.

The table was covered with ancient scrolls and books in languages that Ben could not read. Carter arranged three oil lamps to give them enough light to study by. "My child would have been about the same age as you now," he said.

Ben let that comment slide and picked up one of the volumes, intrigued despite himself. It was a heavy book, obviously several hundred years old. Carefully Ben opened it and began to leaf through the pages. He remembered Jago Moon once telling him about monks who spent their whole lifetime writing and decorating sacred books and he guessed that this tome was something similar. The calligraphy was incredibly intricate, but although he didn't understand the words, Ben could tell that its subject wasn't anything as peaceful as a book of prayers. The illustrations were a hint: Ben guessed that normal monks rarely drew pictures as horrific as these. He closed the book again quickly, but he knew the images would stay with him.

"So what did you want to show me?" he asked.

Claw Carter picked up a scroll and spread it wide, weighing it down with two of the lamps. "It's written in Sumerian," said Carter, with a scholar's enthusiasm. "It was once the possession of a man named Simon Magus, a greatly revered member of the Legion. He was executed for sorcery nearly two thousand years ago. He foresaw that one day a great leader would rise up and strike the decisive blow against the Watchers. I am convinced that the great leader is you, Benjamin Kingdom."

Ben leaned forward, his heart hammering. His eyes were fixed on an illustration in the centre of the scroll. It showed a boy with red hair with his left arm raised and what appeared to be lightning bolts emanating from his fingertips. The boy in the picture was surrounded by the bodies of people he had slain, smoking slightly where his power had struck them.

"The Legion will soon be gathering at the Tower of London for the Feast of Ravens, and it is there, dear Ben, that I want to put my theory to the test. Mr. Sweet intends to crown himself that night, as King of the Legion and then King of the nation. Once, it was my plan to wear that crown myself, but now…" Carter smiled like a wolf in the lamplight. "Now I think that it should be *yours*. Just imagine it! The Hand of Hell wearing the Crown of Corruption – you would become the most devastating power this world has ever known!"

Carter continued to speak but Ben's ears barely registered what he was saying. Ben's eyes ran across the scroll from horror to horror, finally stopping on the image of an old woman, lying dead beneath a mound of stones.

"See anyone you recognize?" asked Carter.

The woman bore an uncanny likeness to Mother Shepherd.

"Why would I want to destroy everything?" said Ben, his voice hardly more than a whisper.

"For the sake of revenge," said Carter.

"Is that enough?"

"It is for me," said Carter matter-of-factly. "Don't you want to punish the One who stole your mother from you?"

The hole inside Ben contracted painfully. Yes, he missed his mother, with all his heart. But was this what she would have wanted for him? Then he thought of Nathaniel, locked up somewhere, soon to be sacrificed. What if the only way to save him was to do Carter's bidding?

Carter was watching him carefully. "Of course," he said conversationally, "there is only one way of testing whether you *are* the chosen one."

"Go on," said Ben, hesitantly.

"I want you to eliminate someone for me, Benjamin," said Carter. "His name is Mr. Sweet."

"If you mean 'kill' him, then say so."

"Yes, Ben," said Carter. "You have to kill Mr. Sweet. I have no doubt you can do it. I already have the bait to lure Sweet out into the open; his dear old battleaxe of a mother is trussed and waiting. All you have to do is allow yourself to be a channel for the power of Hell. You'll enjoy it, I'm sure." Carter met his eyes. "Look inside yourself... you know this is who you are."

DAY FIVE
12TH MARCH, 1892

Chapter 28

Revelations

Ben woke with a start, blinking furiously, his breath coming in short, shallow bursts. He was soaked with sweat, his shirt clinging to his body, his fists knotted tight. It took him a few seconds to make sense of his surroundings. He was in the Under, he realized, in the barracks. And someone was sitting on the edge of his bed.

"Easy now," said a soft voice, "you were having a nightmare."

It came back to Ben in vivid flashes. Two Ben Kingdoms had haunted his dreams: one who tried to do good, but failed every time, and another who did evil and was horribly successful at it.

And in both versions, Nathaniel died.

Ruby handed him a cracked mug of water and Ben drank it gratefully, gulping it down. They were alone in the barracks. Only Alexander Valentine remained, lying stiff in his bed and wheezing like an old man. Ruby went over to him and checked that he was sleeping, pulling his blanket up to protect his weak chest.

"How long were you sitting there?" Ben asked, mopping his lips with the back of his hand.

"Only most of the night," Ruby replied.

"You didn't have to do that."

"I wanted to," said Ruby. "I needed to know if you were still the Ben I used to know."

"So much has happened to both of us, Ruby."

"You're the one they're calling a murderer," she said flatly.

"It didn't happen the way Mickelwhite says," Ben protested. "It was my fault that Mother Shepherd died, but I didn't want it to happen."

Ruby softened as she heard the truth in his words.

"Anyway," said Ben, "you're in the Legion, I thought you would be glad, like the others."

Ruby sighed. Ben watched her fingers trace the Legion Mark branded on her palm. "I'm alone," said Ruby with a crack in her voice. "I have no family. I steal things to survive, and I hide down here with the Legion because it was here or the workhouse."

Ben shuddered; he would rather sleep rough than find himself in the workhouse. He thought too of his own father and the agony he must be going through now that *both* of his sons were missing. For the first time Ben saw a different side to Ruby Johnson. Gone was the confident young lady that she always showed the world, replaced by a sad and lonely girl.

"Why not leave?" Ben asked.

"Easier said than done," said Ruby. "The Legion doesn't let you go without a struggle... If I was going to run, I'd need to have a partner, someone to watch my back." She paused, and glanced around anxiously. "If you wanted to leave, Ben, leave for good this time...I'd go with you."

Ben shook his head. "I don't know where to go any more, Ruby. If Claw Carter is right, then I'm the Hand of Hell and my place is here with the Legion. If he's wrong, then I'm a failure as the Hand of Heaven, and I might as well stay in the Under. I lost control, Ruby, and Mother Shepherd paid for it. The Watchers are better off without me."

"You said it yourself, Ben. Being the Hand is all about choices. So why don't you choose not to be the Hand at all? Live your life for yourself? Not worry about the Watchers or the Legion or anyone else… We could leave London completely, you and I, look after ourselves…"

Ben reacted instinctively. "I'm not going anywhere without Nathaniel."

"Alright," Ruby conceded. "But think about it, Ben—"

Suddenly, Valentine began to gasp for breath, a terrible deep choking which racked his frail body in waves. Spitting blood, the boy struggled to get himself upright on his bunk, spots of bright red dripping onto the front of his nightshirt. Ben couldn't stand to hear his suffering. He went over to Valentine, doing his best to get him into a more comfortable position. But no matter which way the boy sat, the cough refused to release its grasp.

"Quick," said Ben, filled with pity. "Get me another cup of water."

Valentine was in a bad way. Ben could see the blue rivers of his veins through the waxy sheet of his skin. The boy fumbled with the cup, spilling some of the water and lacking the strength to get it to his mouth without Ben's help. Gratefully Valentine took a feeble sip and then the awful convulsions grabbed him again, shaking him like a child with a rattle. Without thinking, Ben put his right hand on Valentine's chest and felt the boy's heart fluttering weakly.

"Take it easy," said Ben softly.

And then Ben's hand began to throb.

It started with pins and needles in his fingers, a tingling sensation which grew until his right hand was pulsing with strange power. Ben closed his eyes and let the energy channel through him; he was the pathway, not the source.

It's not your day to die, Alexander Valentine, Ben thought, a smile spreading across his face as he felt the release of supernatural electricity from his fingertips.

The transformation was remarkable.

For a moment Valentine's spasms grew more intense, as if he were in the throes of a fit. Then they ceased completely. His lungs began to inflate and deflate normally, his chest rose and fell with increasing vigour. The rattle inside his ribcage was silent. His lips slowly changed from deathly blue to pink.

"I say," said Alexander Valentine, sitting up under his own strength for the first time in months. "What did you do to me?"

"Just giving you a hand, mate."

Ben grinned broadly as a revelation struck him with blinding clarity. It was suddenly so obvious. Who he really was. What he was meant to be.

Surely this was what his life should be about? It was not about being a weapon, Ben realized, not for the

Watchers or the Legion. It was about the sort of power that can change the world.

The Hand, thought Ben. *The Right Hand*.

Ruby gazed at Ben with amazement.

"Come on, Ruby," said Ben, grabbing his billycock and shoving it onto his head. "Fetch your coat. We're leaving."

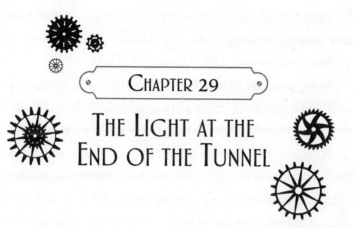

CHAPTER 29

THE LIGHT AT THE END OF THE TUNNEL

"I should have seen it all along," said Ben, as they sneaked through the Under. "The Hand of Heaven doesn't work *for* me, it works *through* me. Don't you see what that means?"

Ruby didn't.

"It means that I can never *make* it work… All the time I thought that I was doing something wrong, or that I wasn't worthy, but it's not like that at all."

"So, do you think you could do that again? Heal someone else, I mean?"

"I don't know," said Ben. "I don't think what *I* want comes into it."

"But think about the possibilities, Ben," said Ruby, her face lighting up. "We could make some money out of this."

Ruby's words turned Ben's thoughts back to the Coin, still lurking malevolently in his pocket.

It was time to get shot of it, once and for all.

It had been a burden from the very start, he saw that now. It was like a magnifying glass which increased every wrong desire that lurked within him. Keeping hold of it was as dangerous as running around with explosives in his pocket. He hated the way that he acted when the Coin's rage and greed erupted inside him and he daren't risk that ever happening again.

He would give the Coin to the Weeping Man and confess everything, he decided. It was the best idea he had come up with in ages. That didn't mean that all his problems were over, however. He still had to find Nathaniel. And then they'd have to actually escape from the Under and make it back to the Watchers... Part of him was dreading that. He knew that he'd have to face Jago Moon and Lucy Lambert and tell them the truth about Mother Shepherd. And ask them for forgiveness. After that?

He knew one thing – Jago Moon had told him often enough – *everyone deserves a second chance*. Surely, even if they didn't want him to be their leader, he could still be a Watcher.

"I think I know which way we should go," Ruby said, holding out her hand.

"Will this lead us to Nathaniel?" Ben asked.

Ruby stopped dead. "I don't know where your brother is, Ben. No one does. Mr. Sweet keeps moving him."

Ben's heart crashed down from the heights it had reached. "I'm not leaving him," said Ben flatly, his mind searching for a solution. "I'll go and see Carter. I'm sure that I can trick him into giving Nathaniel's location away."

"I'm sorry," said Ruby, as gently as she could. "Carter lied to you. Sweet is the *only* one who knows where your brother is."

"Then we'll look for him, you and me." Ben wasn't giving up that easily.

"The Under is vast, Ben. It stretches for miles. We'll never find Nathaniel if Sweet doesn't want us to."

As much as Ben hated it, he realized that Ruby was right.

He would leave now, but he would return...with a plan and with reinforcements. Until then, Nathaniel was at Sweet's mercy.

Munro had always hated Ben Kingdom.

The hunchback had been watching Ben quietly from the shadows since he and Ruby had left the barracks together. A few times Munro thought that he might have been spotted, but he had a talent for hiding. It was something which he had been forced to learn at an early age. Hiding from the other children; hiding from his father.

From the cover of darkness, Munro saw Ben holding Ruby's hand. The pair of them were whispering excitedly. They were so wrapped up in each other that they didn't even glance in his direction.

And they were none the wiser as he hobbled quietly after them.

Not so clever now, are you, Ben Kingdom?

Munro hated Ben's cocky mouth. He hated his red hair. He especially hated the way he was talking to Ruby.

Munro saw the way that Ruby smiled at Ben and he felt as if she was stabbing him in the heart. *Not Ruby.*

Munro was used to being hurt. He was used to being laughed at and scorned. But not by Ruby Johnson. When she looked at him with her big green eyes, it was as if she didn't see his twisted lip, or his partially closed eye, or even the hump which bent his back. Munro had always believed that Ruby Johnson was his friend.

And now Ben Kingdom was stealing her away.

Munro knew from their furtiveness that Ben and Ruby were up to something, but now he saw what they were planning. They had gone down a forbidden tunnel and that could only mean one thing: they were trying to leave the Under in secret.

Munro was faced with the prospect of never seeing Ruby again. He couldn't allow that to happen. He turned and ran as fast as he could, a shambling, lolloping gallop.

It was only his anger that carried him onwards and he was on the verge of collapse when he finally found Claw Carter. He brought himself as erect as he was able before the knight commander, wheezing noisily as he made the Legion salute.

"Spit it out," Carter snapped.

"Ben Kingdom...Ruby Johnson..." Munro forced the words out. "Gone..."

"Gone? Gone where?"

"The Metropolitan," said Munro.

Claw Carter roared.

"So far, so good," said Ruby, keeping her voice down.

Ben had to agree. They had hardly seen a soul so far.

Every step brought him closer to escaping the Under, to

escaping Claw Carter. He thought of the man he had once so admired – a man of great intellect, and great talents – and Ben felt a pang of pity towards him. Ben knew the pain of loss but he also knew that part of Professor Carter had died along with his wife: the man had lost his soul.

Ruby brought them to a locked door and Ben's attention refocused on the stone carving of an angry skull and crossbones. It was a clear message to anyone in the Under, the illiterate included: *Keep Out.* Unperturbed, Ruby had her lock-picks in her hand and winkled the door open in less than a minute.

"I'm impressed," said Ben as they stepped into the sealed passageway, closing the door behind them.

"So you should be," said Ruby.

They were standing in absolute darkness, close enough for Ben to feel Ruby's breath on his skin. "Well, this is cosy," said Ben.

Ruby poked around in her bag until she found a box of lucifers and a stub of candle. She struck the match and in the sudden flare of light they each saw their own smile mirrored on the other's face.

"We aren't allowed to be in this tunnel," said Ruby with glee. "It's prohibited to any Legionnaire below the rank of knight commander."

"Where does it lead to?" asked Ben.

"You'll see," said Ruby.

She went ahead of Ben, lighting the way. The tunnel itself was no different to a hundred others he had seen in the Under; a combination of medieval splendour and Victorian ingenuity. Although he now knew that he didn't belong in this hidden world, Ben couldn't help but be impressed by the vision of Valentine's distant ancestor, the original architect of this secret network, and by all the engineers who had come after him. It was incredible to think that they had built an entire community beneath the London streets. What a shame they hadn't found a better use for it, thought Ben. In spite of all its wonders, it was just another rookery: a place where crime and desperation fed and multiplied.

His feet longed to be back on the surface, walking the dirty cobbles of Old Gravel Lane. No, he thought with a grin, back on the surface and running across the rooftops.

There were no exits from this passage, Ben noticed. It ran in a straight line and then disturbingly Ruby's candle seemed to show that it came to a dead end. That was when Ben spotted the dark circle of the hole in the floor and guessed what was coming next. His suspicions were confirmed when he felt the rumble of an enormous engine rising up from beneath his feet.

They stopped beside the hole and looked down into its black mouth. Ben saw iron rungs embedded in the side of the shaft, and as he peered down a hot wind rushed up to meet him, bringing with it the taste of soot and steam. The distant rumbling became a thunderous roar.

"Tickets, please," said Ruby, still smiling. "This is our express passage out of here, Ben. Don't worry," she reassured him, "I've done this before. I'll give you some advice, though…put on these gloves and hold on tight."

Cautiously at first, Ben followed Ruby down the ladder, hand over hand. A huge cloud of steam and soot filled the narrow shaft and Ben could feel the fierce heat emanating from the train as it passed. A shower of embers from the funnel briefly illuminated Ruby. She was poised at the bottom of the vertical tunnel with nothing beneath her except the morning train on the Metropolitan line.

"You can't be serious," Ben shouted.

"Follow me!" Ruby yelled above the thunder of the pistons.

Ben watched as she dropped, catlike, onto the roof of a passenger carriage and was swept away out of sight. The huge iron wheels sparked as they shrieked against the rails. He knew that he only had seconds if he was going to catch the train with her.

Ruby had made it look easy. *She makes* everything *look easy*, Ben thought. He shuffled into position and then…

It's now or never, he decided, and he let himself drop.

Ben landed heavily on his hands and knees and immediately scrambled to find a grip on the smooth carriage roof. The train charged through the darkness. Ben fumbled blindly, desperate for something, *anything*, that he could get a grasp on. *This gets better and better*, he thought as a bend in the tunnel made the whole train tilt to the left and Ben was flung to the edge of the roof. He wasn't sure how he managed to find a handhold but he clung to it like grim death.

Looking forward along the length of the train, Ben could make out Ruby in the red glow of the firebox. He got a better grip and as he started to feel more confident a smile spread across his face.

They were leaving the Under, leaving the Legion; for ever this time. Ben tugged his billycock hat down tight to stop the wind in the tunnel from whipping it off. There was every chance he could be moments away from falling from the train and being mangled beneath it, but he felt vigorously and wonderfully alive. This was escaping in style!

The lantern on the front of the engine pierced the darkness ahead of them and Ben fancied that he saw

Ruby's emerald eyes as she looked back at him. He counted six carriages between them and carefully began to crawl towards her, praying all the while that he could hold on until the tunnel broke the surface.

It wasn't easy going.

Ben had to keep low to save himself from being dashed against the tunnel roof, and the train swayed alarmingly every time it came to a curve in the tracks. He wondered if he might be better off climbing down *between* the carriages and taking shelter there, if he could make it that far. He might even try the door and introduce himself in first class; no doubt they would be delighted to meet him.

Meanwhile the noise in the tunnel was deafening. Ruby was shouting something to him but he couldn't make out the words. He watched her lips carefully.

Behind.

You.

With a sinking feeling, Ben looked over his shoulder.

The whole train was covered with Feathered Men.

Ben had to fight down his panic as he watched the fallen angels advance towards him along the roof of the train. He should have known that Claw Carter wouldn't let them out of his clutches that easily.

Illuminated by the flames from the engine and the sparks from the wheels, Ben saw brief glimpses of beaks silently opening and closing in anticipation. Several of the winged demons were actually flying down the tunnel, staying close to the train to avoid colliding with the low roof.

One landed, using its savage claws to puncture the roof of the carriage just behind him. As quickly as he dared, Ben scrabbled onwards towards the cab and Ruby. He just managed to reach the end of the compartment when he felt elongated fingers encircle his ankle. He turned to look, and the Feathered Man gave a shriek that stripped away all hope.

With nothing left inside him except desperation and defiance, Ben kicked savagely with his free foot. He tried to scrape his heel against the creature's bony knuckles, and stamp in its inhuman face. The Feathered Man gave a croaking laugh which only spurred Ben on to lash out more violently. *If I'm going down, I'm going down fighting...*

More by chance than design, one of his blows managed to strike the Feathered Man in the eye and this time it didn't laugh it off; it howled with pain. As it lifted its talons to protect its face, it released Ben from its grasp. Ben saw his chance and scrambled forwards, anxious to put some distance between them. Unfortunately, his lucky blow didn't buy him more than a couple of seconds.

With one bloodshot eye, the enraged Feathered Man

threw itself towards Ben, intent on revenge. Sensing the attack, Ben rolled onto his back, drawing his knees towards his chest in the hope of fending the beast off again with his boots.

The Feathered Man landed on top of him and Ben found himself holding the creature's entire weight on his feet. Surprised to have its attack halted, the hideous creature strained its neck, keen to reach Ben's face with its snapping beak. Ben could feel the muscles in his legs burning with the effort of holding the monster back and he knew that he couldn't keep it at bay for much longer. Summoning all his hidden reserves of strength, Ben gave a mighty heave with both legs and launched the Feathered Man up into the air...and into the roof of the tunnel. Ben held it there for a second whilst the bricks did their bloody work, and then the creature was gone in a mess of tangled wings.

He watched it tumble away from him down the length of the carriage. In its agony, it flailed around uncontrollably and managed to unseat two of its brothers from the roof in the process. They too fell from the train and into the oblivion of the tunnel. But there was no jubilation for Ben.

Three Feathered Men had been defeated, but in their place he could count at least a dozen more, smothering the roof and sides of the train compartments like some sort of plague. They were angry. And every single one of them was looking at him.

CHAPTER 30

DEATH IN THE DARK

Inside the train, Reginald Cowper, junior clerk and Sunday school teacher, felt afraid. He ran his finger around the inside of his starched collar. It was too tight, too stiff. There was nothing to stop him from loosening his tie and making himself feel more comfortable and yet he hesitated. It was not the done thing. He was an Englishman, Cowper told himself firmly. It was important to keep up appearances.

That was what he was doing now, he and the other subdued passengers on the train, going about their business as if London hadn't changed. He kept going because that was what Englishmen did. Stiff upper lip and all that.

He lived near the station, which made it easier for him, he supposed, although he still had to shuffle every step of the way, using the railings to guide him in the appalling fog. There had been no one behind the desk at the ticket counter but Cowper slipped the money over the desk anyway. It had been especially quiet on the platform, the other commuters hardly daring to make eye contact. That was except for an unfortunate madman, who shook and trembled and raved about bird-headed demons, until eventually he climbed off the platform and onto the tracks, running down the tunnel, screaming as he went. That encounter had shaken Cowper to the core. He was afraid of demons.

He had taught his Sunday school class about them: horrible, evil creatures – the demons, not his class – but he had never truly expected to meet one. Mrs. Troughton, who worked in the post office on the corner and played the organ at chapel every other Sunday, said that her sister Mary's boy Alfie had spoken to a chimney sweep who was almost positive that he saw one up on the rooftops before all this terrible business started. That was quite close enough, as far as Reginald Cowper was concerned.

The train shuddered violently and Cowper was flung sideways in his seat. He was sitting beside a somewhat severe-looking woman and to his horror his head actually landed in the soft cushion of her lap. He didn't know which of them was the most mortified and he began to apologize profusely, when the compartment rocked again and he was thrown in the opposite direction.

"I'm so sorry," he tried again, but then his attention was drawn to crashing sounds coming from the roof of the train. Every frightened eye looked upwards.

It wasn't possible, of course. It couldn't possibly be footsteps…

But that's all it can be, Cowper realized with sickening dread, as he listened to the steady *thump, thump, thump* above his head.

He was so distracted by the ominous sound that he didn't notice the creature that was clinging to the side of his compartment and observing him through the window – until the stern woman screamed.

Cowper didn't scream. He didn't have time. A pair of long hands smashed through the pane and dragged him out into the darkness.

A scream pierced the roaring of the tunnel.

Ben could see a Feathered Man bearing down on Ruby. It must have clambered along the side of the train.

He had never seen such raw emotion in her green eyes.

Ben brought himself up into a low crouch and tried to think fast, whilst thick clouds of smoke eddied around him. He needed to do something quickly. Especially because a particularly nasty-looking specimen, with a battle-scarred beak and a missing talon on one hand was almost on top of him. Three Fingers had a heartless gaze. It wanted him dead, Ben knew.

He found the courage to try standing, and discovered that his skyboots actually made walking a better option than crawling. *Provided I keep my head down*, thought Ben, remembering the Feathered Man who had been dashed to pieces against the roof.

Three Fingers continued to advance. Ben rolled his hand into a fist, then thought better of it. He turned and, after a second to get used to the drunken yawing of the train, broke into a low run.

Ruby was terrified. He could see her on the coal wagon, scrambling backwards over the heap of coal, trying to keep the Feathered Man at bay.

Ben reached the end of his compartment and faltered. The jump to the next carriage was one that he could easily have made if he was up on the surface. But here, in the dark, at speed, with no headroom, it was a different matter. Behind him Three Fingers hissed and made up

Ben's mind for him. Ben leaped forward. Three Fingers slashed at him but its claws passed through empty air.

"Hold on, Ruby," Ben yelled. "I'm coming."

Now that he was getting the hang of it, Ben quickly closed the gap between him and Ruby. The Feathered Man was hunched over her, its beak snapping spitefully. Without hesitation Ben threw a swinging punch, which caught the fallen angel squarely on the side of the head and sent it staggering.

"Get away from her!" Ben shouted.

Ben knew that he couldn't allow the Feathered Man a second to recover. While it was still disorientated, Ben stepped in as close as he dared and gave a mighty double-handed shove. It was enough to knock the fallen angel off its feet and send it skittering over the side of the train.

Ruby fell into Ben's arms. For a split second she let her mask of confidence slip, revealing the scared street kid she worked so hard to keep hidden.

"Come on," said Ben. "Let's see if we can make it to the cab."

"What is it with boys?" said Ruby, making a show of freeing herself from his arms, keen to put on her old act again. "You always want to be train drivers."

"You don't have to pretend with me, Ruby," said Ben as

they scrambled over the mountain of coal in the tender. "Not any more."

Ruby didn't say another word.

When Ben swung into the cab of the train, the driver and his fireman were waiting to greet him. The driver had adopted a stance like a boxer, his fists raised and making menacing circles in the air, while his feet did a nervous dance. The fireman, a huge man, naked to the waist and drenched in sweat, clutched his coal shovel like an axe.

"What's your game?" the driver blustered. "What are those...*things* you've brought onto my train?"

Ben didn't have time for explanations. "How do you make this train go faster?" he asked as Ruby clambered in behind him.

The driver looked at the gauge. "Faster? We're going nearly thirty-four miles an hour already!"

"We're under attack," said Ben. "I need you to crank this engine up as fast as it can go if we're going to shake those monsters off."

Another scream echoed down the tunnel and the fireman began to fling coals into the furnace as if his life depended on it. Which, of course, it did.

"And what if we can't, what happens th—"

The driver's question went unfinished as two long-fingered hands were clamped over his mouth. A Feathered

Man looked in at Ben, cocked its head and then, with a quick twist of its wrists, snapped the man's neck and tossed him out onto the track. The fireman responded swiftly, raising his shovel and hefting it at the Feathered Man like a club. It was a good swing, Ben thought, as the fallen angel staggered from the force of the blow. But before the man could attack again, the Feathered Man picked him up as easily as a father carrying a child and threw him out of the cab too.

Ruby screamed and shrank behind Ben for protection. Thinking on his feet, Ben snatched up the shovel where the poor fireman had dropped it, but he didn't repeat the stoker's mistake. Instead he shoved it deep into the firebox and pulled out a heap of burning coals, which he threw at the Feathered Man. The air was filled with the acrid stench of burning feathers and for a horrible second they watched the creature fighting to quench the flames on its wings before it too fell onto the track and disappeared.

Hugging each other for comfort, Ben and Ruby slumped to the floor. They could hear thuds and scratching as more clawed feet advanced towards them along the roof of the train.

In panic, Ben's thoughts turned to the Judas Coin. *It's now or never*. He had to be rid of the Coin before the Feathered Men got their clutches on it.

For a second he considered simply throwing the Coin out into the tunnel, but how much time would that win for the Watchers? A day? A week? A year? No time at all if a Feathered Man spotted him throwing it. No. Ben knew that would not stop the Legion from getting their most sought-after prize.

It was like an oven inside the cab and a bead of sweat made the journey down Ben's forehead and slipped, stinging, into his eye. *Yes*, he thought as he blinked away the pain. *That just might work, if I'm quick about it.*

Ben reached into his pocket for the Coin. *It's hot where you're going*, he thought as he aimed it at the waiting mouth of the firebox… But he was stopped by the long thin arms that wrapped around him and the rasping voice that gurgled in his ear.

"Claw Carter is disappointed in you," hissed the Feathered Man.

"Well, you can tell him that the feeling is mutual," Ben replied.

Without a driver to apply the brakes, the train was hurtling through the darkness at a reckless pace and as they swung into a bend, the whole engine lurched over at an alarming angle. Ben doubted whether it would stay on the tracks if it hit another steep curve.

The train momentarily righted itself as they hit a

straight length and Ben took his chance.

He flicked his wrist and sent the Judas Coin spinning in a neat arc.

All three sets of eyes followed its path, captivated.

A small spinning disc of silver...

An object of unimaginable evil and power...

Destined for oblivion in the flames...

And it would have been destroyed, if Ruby hadn't intercepted it.

Behind him the Feathered Man screamed in recognition and began to squeeze the life out of Ben's body.

Ruby looked down at the Coin in her hand, and Ben felt something break inside him as he saw the emotions written on her face.

Those beautiful emerald eyes grew wide at first and then narrowed into tiny slits.

"It's mine," she breathed.

Then a Feathered Man reached in and plucked her away, leaving Ben with the memory of the friend he had lost.

She was gone for ever.

CHAPTER 31

THE END OF THE LINE

The train was out of control.

It was careening along the tracks at a bone-rattling speed, tilting more dangerously with every bend.

They were going to crash and everyone would die if Ben didn't do something to stop it.

Ben and the Feathered Man were sent staggering as they hit another corner. As the fallen angel loosened its grip, Ben seized his chance. He dived forward, grabbed the shovel and then spun, hammering it against the creature's wing, feeling the snap of bone. The Feathered Man issued a hideous scream of pain. He hit it again and again, aiming at its legs, until it slumped in the corner, cradling its broken limbs.

Ben didn't know how to drive a train. He had only ridden in one once before in his life and although he had hung around the freight yards with the other boys from Old Gravel Lane, their main interest had been how much coal they could nick without getting caught, rather than learning the finer details of how to work a steam engine. He scanned the array of dials and gauges and quickly found a circle of brass with a protruding handle, helpfully labelled *brake*, and with two positions marked *ON* and *OFF*.

Ben pushed the handle from *OFF* to *ON*. Nothing happened.

The fallen angel slumped in the corner started to make an ugly croaking sound.

"Think it's funny, do you?" said Ben through gritted teeth. He looked around for an alternative option and settled on a large lever rising up out of the floor of the cab. It was angled forward. Ben took it in both hands, released the catch and pulled back hard, hoping for the best.

A grinding sound rose up from beneath them. At least the lever did something, Ben thought. As they shuddered over a set of points, the whole train vibrated with such violence that Ben was amazed it didn't jump the tracks. He pulled back even harder, making the sinews stand proud on his arms.

It wasn't going to be enough.

Ben could hear the terrified cries of the passengers behind him in the carriages and he redoubled his efforts. Screwing up his face against the pain, he strained on the handle and felt it ease back a fraction of an inch more…

I'm doing it, thought Ben. Then they hit another set of points and, just as he had feared, he felt the train tremble as one set of wheels was thrown off.

The noise was incredible as the train shook itself free from the rails. Metal raged against metal. Sparks flew. Waves of gravel began to fly up as the engine ploughed on.

Ben wasn't trying to stop the train now. He was just trying to stay alive.

The engine car was scraping along the tunnel wall, sending up clouds of masonry dust and a steady rain of bricks. Pipes started to explode somewhere inside the great engine and filled the air with a hissing, like the final breath of some huge beast. The Feathered Man had stopped its croaking laughter and sheltered itself beneath its unbroken wing.

Incredibly, the train staggered to a halt. Shaking with emotion, Ben put his head out of the cab and looked back up the tunnel. Although the carriages were balanced at precarious angles, not one of them had toppled over.

The Feathered Man struggled to its feet and regarded Ben with its cold bird-eyes. For the first time ever, Ben saw one of the creatures blink.

"Yeah," said Ben. "You and me both."

It was then that Three Fingers emerged from the darkness with a hiss, blocking the cab door and his means of escape. Behind him, Broken Wing covered the other exit. Ben was trapped. He raised the shovel to defend himself, but Three Fingers swept it from his grasp and flung itself upon him. Ben struggled in vain as he was swept up into the fallen angel's arms and carried away past the wreckage. There was no escape for him today.

CHAPTER 32

THE
WATCHER SPY

Claw Carter looked down at the small piece of silver sitting in the palm of his hand. Was it worth it? he wondered. All the years of scheming, all the crimes committed? Yes! came the resounding reply. He would do it all again, and more!

The last Coin of Judas was his.

"So Ruby Johnson gave this to you of her own free will?" he asked Grey Wing sceptically.

"More or less," Grey Wing replied.

"And where is Ruby now?" He had always had a fondness for the girl.

"Contemplating her loss."

"And the hunchback, what's his name?"

"Mourning Miss Johnson's predicament."

Carter nodded, losing interest. Absolutely enthralled by the glint of silver. He could feel the Coin pulling at him already, whispering to the deepest parts of his mind. The fact that Grey Wing could give it up without a second thought highlighted once again the difference between men and fallen angels; only men think metal is worth fighting over, the fallen angel had once told him.

"And Sweet knows nothing of it, you're certain?" Carter asked.

"I do not answer to any man unless I choose to," said Grey Wing. "And my feathered brothers follow *my* lead."

Carter nodded again, pleased that their alliance was holding strong, for now.

"And Ben Kingdom?"

"It was not possible to keep his arrival in the Under a secret. He kept shouting that he was the Hand of Heaven."

What else should he have expected? Ben always did have a loud mouth.

"And so Sweet has him?"

"He has been taken to the Tower. Sweet will execute him at the Feast," said Grey Wing.

Carter felt an unexpected stab inside his own heart. He remembered that he had once promised Ben Kingdom the chance to travel with him and see the world. At the time Carter had been lying, naturally; merely flattering the boy to make him easier to manipulate, but now…the prospect was actually an appealing one. There were so many more treasures that he still wanted to search for, after he had resolved his differences with Mr. Sweet, of course. All the books he had read, all the wisdom he had accumulated… he had dared to imagine that he might have an heir to pass them down to at last.

"So," he declared, after a moment of reflection. "You know what comes next, don't you?"

Grey Wing nodded once and his eyes grew wide with anticipation.

"It is time for you and I to make our move," said Carter.

Unseen and unmissed, Munro sat in the barracks in the Under. He cradled Buster in his arms, the three-legged dog breaking wind softly.

"I'm sorry, Miss Ruby," he mumbled, hugging Buster closer. "I only wanted you to stay with me. I didn't know they would do that to you… I never meant…" Munro's words dissolved into sobbing.

No one heard him. No one cared.

"He's late," said Lucy.

"Very late," Moon agreed.

Their journey to the rendezvous had been slow and dangerous. Feathered Men circled the sky, armed soldiers patrolled the streets. On the rooftops the Watchers were open and exposed, on the ground they were target practice. Exhausted, they managed to grab an hour's sleep in a Watcher safe house on Coldbath Square, and now they were holed up in a damp cellar that smelled of rotting potatoes and despair.

Lucy was cold. She found some old canvas sacking and draped it round her shoulders like a blanket. Ghost paced restlessly back and forth, like a caged panther. Moon positioned himself in a battered armchair.

"But we wait," said Moon, tapping the wooden lid with his cane. "Our agent inside the Legion has never let us down before."

Providing his cover hasn't been blown, he thought bleakly.

Moon's body felt stiff and he shifted in his chair, trying and failing to make himself more comfortable. The war was taking its toll on them and they would need all their strength before the day was won or lost. They had been living on adrenaline and prayers, and they were running short of both.

272

At last Moon heard the sound that he had been listening for: the subtle groan of wooden rungs as they took the weight of a climber, followed by the whisper of the trapdoor lifting.

"Mr. Moon!" said the boy with obvious relief. "I hope I have not kept you waiting long."

"Only as long as necessary, lad," said Moon warmly. He liked this Watcher, and admired him too. There was great courage in the Watcher life; to put self last and live for others, to make your home among the chimneys and steeples. There was even greater bravery though, in his opinion, to live the Watcher life in the company of the Legion.

Lucy and Ghost woke as they heard the voices. "Hans!" said Lucy as she recognized him. "Are you all right? You look tired."

Hans Schulman pushed his long fair hair away from his face and rubbed his scalp vigorously. "These days are not so good for any of us, I think."

"So," said Moon, getting straight to the point. "Have you got news of Ben?"

"He is not dead yet," Hans replied.

"That doesn't sound good," said Lucy.

"He has been most very brave," said Hans, his German mother tongue showing. "He tried to escape but he was caught, and Mr. Sweet brought him before the ranks of the Legion. Mr. Sweet tried to make Ben abandon the Watchers, but Ben defied him..." Schulman's voice dropped to a whisper. "Mr. Sweet made many firm efforts to persuade him, but Ben only shouted louder '*I am the Hand of Heaven!*'"

Lucy could only imagine what Ben must have been through. She pictured his defiance and she fought back a tear of pride.

Hans paused, a cloud passing over his face. "They are saying things in the Under. Things about Ben and the Great Mother. Are they more Legion lies?"

"No," said Moon, "Mother Shepherd is dead. But, and I want you to be clear on this, Mother Shepherd took the blame for everything that happened. With her dying breath *she* asked for *Ben's* forgiveness."

"Well," said Hans, nodding in understanding, "that is good enough for me."

"So," said Moon. "Do you know where Ben and Nathaniel are being held? Is there any chance that we could get them out?"

Hans shook his head. "Mr. Sweet keeps moving them, only he knows where they are."

"But we know where they will be soon," said Lucy.

"At the Tower of London," Hans confirmed. "Sweet

intends to execute Ben and Nathaniel at the Feast of Ravens. Will the Liberator be ready in time?"

Moon sucked in his breath between brown and crooked teeth. "It's not finished yet," he admitted. "There have been some setbacks. One of the engines blew when Jonas was testing it; some of the hull got shattered into the bargain."

"Then we persevere in faith," said Hans with determination.

Ghost slapped him heartily on the shoulder and the two Watcher boys exchanged a deep look. "We are in agreement," said Hans, with a grin. "We are not slaves to fear."

"Well said," Moon agreed.

"I must return now," said Hans. "If I am gone too long then the others might get suspicious. But before I go, I must give you these." He reached inside his backpack and pulled out a bundle of black cloth, which he passed to Lucy. "I am sure that you will be able to put them to good use, yes."

"Thank you," said Lucy, hugging him close. "Stay safe."

"And you," said Hans, and with that he descended into the tunnel and was gone.

"So," said Moon as he shut the trapdoor.

"So," said Lucy. "It looks like were going to have to rescue our great leader yet again."

CHAPTER 33

WICKED WORK

Claw Carter was a hunter and he knew how to set a trap. It didn't have to be elaborate; providing you used the right bait, your prey would come to you. He had seen the wiliest Bengal tigers lured to their death by nothing more than a juicy goat staked out and begging to be eaten. Mr. Sweet might think that he was cunning, but he was an animal beneath that veneer. Just like those tigers, Sweet would wander out into the open and – *BANG!* – Carter would put a bullet between his eyes.

If Ben had joined him, then this would have been his initiation. As it was the task fell to Carter himself. He would take no special pleasure in the kill. This was not personal; he didn't need to do the deed up close. Mr. Sweet was merely an obstacle who had stood in his way for too long.

Carter lay on the deck of the Thames steamboat, peering through the telescopic sight of his rifle. It was a unique weapon, built to his own design. The stock fitted snugly into the pit of his shoulder, as with a normal rifle, but a precision-made niche allowed him to support the weight of the gun with his claw, leaving his human hand to pull the trigger.

Calmly, Carter observed the elderly woman tied to Cleopatra's Needle on the Victoria Embankment. It was the perfect location, he thought. Now that the fog had done its wicked work, bringing London under Legion control, its grip on the city was no longer needed. Down along the river's edge, it was already beginning to thin. That meant that whichever direction Sweet came from to rescue this dear grey-haired lady, cover was virtually non-existent and Sweet would be open and exposed. Lady Honoraria Sweet made for a very juicy goat indeed.

Surely Mr. Sweet would come running for his own mother?

In his vantage point on the steam-launch, Carter shifted position slightly, careful not to disturb the grey canvas sheet which covered him completely. He was content that his knowledge of camouflage was sufficient to render him virtually invisible. That was of the utmost importance because if there was one fact that Carter knew for certain, it was that he would only get one shot. If he missed completely or only wounded Sweet, then the reprisals would be terrible.

For that same reason it had been important that Carter lay down a false scent to lead the trail of suspicion away from him. He had made the kidnapping look like the work of a professional, leaving the ransom note unsigned but marked with a bloody handprint. Sweet would get the message.

If you want her back, bring one thousand pounds to the Needle at five p.m. today. Come alone.

Carter smiled. *Here, kitty, kitty.*

It was a disappointment that Ben was not by his side. Carter remembered hunting with his own father, a long time ago now...

Like every good hunter, Carter was patient when it came to waiting for the kill. Just for a second, he took his finger away from the gun and flexed his hand. He wanted to make sure that he had complete control when the time came. He returned his finger to the trigger and there it sat comfortably, without even the slightest tremor.

Carter counted down the minutes. The deadline was

drawing near and he knew that Sweet would not risk being late.

Five o'clock.

Carter squinted down the barrel of his rifle, taking a bead through the telescopic sight. He scanned for movement, *any movement*, that might give Sweet's position away. Would he come from the left or the right along the embankment?

The slightest groaning of a plank on the steamboat's deck told Carter that he was not alone. Someone was behind him. He had been outmanoeuvred.

A single shot rang out; a crack which broke the unnatural calm and sent a raven squawking into the air. Lady Honoraria Sweet's head dropped limply onto her chest.

But Carter's finger had not pulled the trigger.

He could hear soft footsteps behind him and yet he dared not turn his head.

"Father?" said a thin voice, which brought Carter's arms up in goose pimples. "Father, is that you?"

It sounded like a child. Still clutching his rifle and trying not to tremble, Carter rose to his feet.

"You," he said as he saw the figure standing before him, dressed in a sailor's suit, like a good boy on his way to church.

He had been wrong to summon this being in the first place, Carter saw that now. Mr. Sweet was the only one who had benefited from the Nightmare Child's presence and that had definitely *not* been Carter's plan. Because he had found that he was relatively at ease in the company of the Feathered Men, Carter had wrongly assumed that this fallen cherub would be equally amenable and open to his suggestions. He had been very wrong on that score. The Nightmare Child was a law unto itself.

"Papa," said the Nightmare Child, in a sickly-sweet and wheedling tone. "Why did you leave me and mother in the desert? Why didn't you bring us home with you?"

"Stop this," Carter snapped. "Stop this at once!"

"Don't be cross, Papa," the cherub continued. "I love you."

Carter felt the unnatural power as the fallen angel spoke. The words resounded inside his head and he felt his legs begin to give way beneath him as the line between reality and fantasy started to blur. "Stop it! You're not my son!"

"Of course I'm not, silly," said the beautiful woman whose photograph he examined every day. "It's me. Don't you know your own wife, James?"

Claw Carter gazed at her face; she was just as exquisite as he remembered her. Hesitantly he reached out to touch her hair. It was like silk. He wanted to bring it to his face and hold it against his cheek.

"Charlotte," he said, as his mind blundered over the edge into insanity, "is it really you?"

"You know it is," she said, her face falling away to show the skull beneath. "Come and give me a kiss."

Mr. Sweet was feeling supremely satisfied.

Claw Carter had been suitably punished. Ben Kingdom was his prisoner. He was in possession of all thirty Coins of Judas. And his pain of a mother was finally off his back for good.

Today he was the Prime Minister. Tomorrow he would place the completed Crown of Corruption on his head and he would become the King. King of the Legion and King of Great Britain.

Since Lord Cecil no longer required his rooms at the Savoy, Sweet had moved in and was making the most of his predecessor's hospitality. He remembered that there was a particularly fine box of cigars on the desk and he reached for one now.

"Just what do you think you're doing, young man?" came a haughty voice that he knew all too well. "I've told you before that those disgusting things are bad for you."

Sweet saw his mother standing in the corner. His dead mother.

"Oliver," she said in a tone full of admonishment, "you have been a very naughty boy indeed."

"Stop this, Moloch! I know it's you." Sweet's own voice rose to a booming crescendo to cover his fear. "*I command you to stop!*"

Before his eyes, Lady Sweet's form melted away to leave the Nightmare Child standing in her place. Smiling.

"I'll stop for now," said the Nightmare Child, speaking once again in the disconcerting high-pitched voice of a small boy. "But I'm bored." It ran to the door, then paused halfway out. "You *will* play my game one day though. Everybody does."

The tiny footsteps pattered away up the corridor, leaving Mr. Sweet chilled to the bone.

DAY SIX
13TH MARCH –
THE FEAST OF RAVENS, 1892

CHAPTER 34

THE FEAST OF RAVENS

Ben gazed up at the Tower of London: a stark silhouette against the tattered remnants of the fog. He shuddered. It was a cold monument with a dark and bloodstained history and he was certain that the Legion was about to write its own gruesome chapter. Ben was their prisoner and he could expect no mercy. The Yeoman Warders were long gone, the Queen was missing, and there were rumours that Mr. Sweet had already helped himself to the Crown Jewels. Only the ravens remained to see Ben's fate, joined by hundreds of Legionnaires gathered for the Feast.

"Keep moving," grunted Ben's guard, a huge man with only two teeth in his mouth, jabbing him in the back for good measure. Ben had no choice but to obey; his hands were tied firmly in front of him. It had been the same story all day, as he had been bundled, helpless, from pillar to post; Mr. Sweet's most treasured prisoner. In his mind Ben had sought the company of Nathaniel and his pa, Lucy and Mr. Moon…Mother Shepherd, but even those familiar faces were too painful for him to bear. Standing there now Ben felt small and lost – surrounded by wickedness on all sides.

The guard halted him at the edge of the crowd as Mr. Sweet's voice echoed across the courtyard. Ben listened in silence.

"My loyal Legionnaires, feast, make merry, for today we begin our reign!"

There was something unreal about the celebration that was going on around him. Although the night air was bitterly cold, there was a festive atmosphere, full of laughter and merriment. The wine and beer were flowing freely and the air was rich with the fatty goodness of roasting pigs; Christmas for evil people, thought Ben. He looked over to one of the cooking fires with longing and watched the hog slowly turning on a spit, the smoke twisting upwards and merging with the dying remnants of the mist. Ben's own stomach was aching with emptiness. To really rub salt in the wound, Ben's guard hadn't stopped shoving juicy slabs of meat into his mouth. *Hope you choke on it*, Ben thought charitably.

Many of the throng had come dressed for the occasion, Ben observed. The women had plaited long black feathers into their hair and some of the men had them too, in their hair or beards. Others were wearing the cowls that Legionnaires often adopted for their surface missions, heavy woollen hoods that cast their faces in shadow. Almost all of the revellers had smeared their faces with broad stripes of black grease; it was a disturbing effect. Most Legionnaires were pretty threatening in a good light, but here, in the flickering glow of the torches, they appeared diabolical.

Ben caught glimpses of staring white eyes and flashing teeth in blackened faces, expressions growing increasingly wild as the drinking slipped over into drunkenness. Someone in the crowd had brought a drum and was beating out a strange rhythm, while the women spun around and shrieked in a wild dance. If it was a party, thought Ben, then it was the sort of party which ended in a fight. He could taste the violence in the air, sour and rank.

Presiding over it all was Mr. Sweet, flanked by a huge pair of Feathered Men. These fallen angels were bigger than most; their feathers were as dark as midnight, their beaks longer – a hideous combination of raven and man. Sweet himself was wearing a magnificent cloak of blue-black feathers which swept out behind him, and although he had not daubed his face, his eyes had the same glassy look of danger. He was standing with his two guards on a raised wooden stage, a lot like the platforms used in public hangings, Ben thought.

Ben's eyes went wide as he saw what else Mr. Sweet had brought with him.

There was a stone plinth on the stage, topped with a rich velvet cushion. And on top of the cushion was a crown. A crown made of silver coins. A crown which radiated pure evil. Ben shuddered. He knew how much dark power a *single* Coin had contained, how terribly one had influenced his actions. But thirty?

"Bring the sacrifice forward!" Sweet ordered.

"That's your cue," Ben's guard gloated.

The crowd parted and Ben was pushed towards the platform. Faces loomed at him from every side, curses and threats on their breath. Something hot and wet landed on Ben's cheek and he realized, to his disgust, that one of the Legionnaires had spat on him.

Numb, Ben stumbled up the wooden steps until he was only a few feet away from Mr. Sweet and the Crown of Corruption.

"See the last hope of the Watchers!" Sweet shouted. "See how he trembles before me!"

Ben remained silent, his mouth dry.

"String him up," said Sweet.

With that, the guard bundled Ben forwards until he was standing beneath the waiting arm of the gibbet. Gleefully, the burly Legionnaire produced a length of rope, fastened one end to Ben's already bound wrists and then threw the other end over the wooden frame. Taking the rope in both hands, the guard heaved downwards and Ben felt his arms being dragged up until he was balanced painfully on tiptoes. The guard then tied the rope off, leaving Ben dangling.

The crowd roared their approval.

Mr. Sweet strode over to Ben and leaned in close, so that he could whisper in his ear. "I hope you have a good view," he said. "I wouldn't want you to miss this."

Sweet returned to centre stage. "Now let me show you how we treat our enemies…"

An arched door opened at the foot of one of the towers and a strange procession filed out. Ben could see a cage, being carried at shoulder height by four Legionnaires and inside it was—

"Nathaniel!" Ben shouted.

"He can't hear you," said Sweet. "He probably doesn't even know who you are any more."

Ben could only watch as other figures trailed behind his brother. He struggled to understand what he was seeing.

The procession was led by the sinister child that Ben had encountered in the fog, followed by what appeared to be a massive hound. No; Ben looked again. Not a dog – a man, on his hands and knees with a leash around his neck.

The Legionnaires roared with anger. "Traitor! Traitor! Traitor!" rang the chant. They screamed at the crawling figure until the veins stood proud on their necks. They spat at him vehemently. "Here, doggie, doggie," mocked one woman, throwing a lump of greasy meat onto the grass in front of the pitiful victim.

Ben almost didn't recognize the poor wretch. The man was insensible. He looked so disorientated, his hair awry, his expression slack. He probably wouldn't recognize his own face in the mirror if he saw it.

It was the claw that gave him away.

"Professor Carter," Ben breathed in disbelief.

"This is what happens to those who betray the Legion," Sweet gloated. "Would you like to see a demonstration of Legion justice in action?"

The mob roared their approval.

"*All praise the Nightmare Child.*"

Sweet slapped his fist to his chest in the Legion salute

and a thousand Legionnaires beat their own chests in response.

Ben ran his eyes across the turrets and the battlements, hoping, praying, to see a Watcher on the rooftops. But he was alone.

Ben didn't want to die – he guessed that *he* was to be the sacrifice now.

Nathaniel was only a few feet away from him, but it may as well have been a mile. The cage that held his brother had been placed at the other end of the stage.

"Nathaniel!" Ben called to him again, but Nathaniel gazed at him as if he were a stranger.

Ben looked again at Professor Carter and saw the same emptiness in his eyes. The man's great intellect had been stolen from him, leaving him no better than a gibbering imbecile. No matter how ruthless the man had been, nobody deserved this fate. Unexpectedly, Ben's heart went out to Carter. If, in his grief, Carter had chosen to follow the Watchers rather than the Legion, how different the man's life might have been.

Choices and consequences, Ben…

Ben didn't understand how Carter could have been reduced to such a pitiful state but he had the sinking feeling that he was about to find out.

The Nightmare Child mounted the stage. In the ugly

sky above, circling ravens croaked in triumph. A few Feathered Men flew with them. All around Ben, the Feast night fires burned intensely, making shadows of every face. It was as if the crowd had become a single being, with one purpose, one black heart. Eating but never satisfied. Drinking without merriment, only as a passage to oblivion. A savage creature made of hair and feathers and hatred, and with a thousand hungry eyes fixed on him.

At the front of the crowd Ben spotted Mickelwhite's face, animated with cruel delight. Beside him, Bedlam was gnawing on a fatty chunk of meat, his lips grinning and glistening, the grease spilling down over his chin. Hans Schulman and Alexander Valentine were there too, looking on impassively.

The mob fell into an expectant hush, until the silence was broken by a barrel-chested Legionnaire in the front row. The man had a beard bristling with feathers, and *HATE* tattooed inexpertly across both sets of knuckles.

"Death to the Watchers!" he yelled and Ben shrank inside himself as the terrible cry was taken up around the Tower. "Death! Death! Death!"

The small blond boy crossed the platform to inspect Ben, looking for another pet to torment. Only it *wasn't* a cruel child, Ben understood. This time, without the fog to blur his sight, he saw the small pair of black wings that sprouted through slits in the shoulders of the sailor suit. Yes, it was something much, much worse.

"What do you want?" Ben asked, doing his best to sound defiant.

"I want to be your friend," said the Nightmare Child. "Will you play a game with me?"

"Sorry," said Ben. "I don't play with girls."

"Oh," said the Nightmare Child, a pink tongue emerging from behind the Cupid's bow of its lips. "This *is* going to be fun."

The fallen cherub regarded Ben with a look of pure malice. Its eyes were dark, almost black, and overflowing with malevolence. Although Ben tried feverishly to look away, he felt himself pulled irresistibly into those inky pools. It was as if he was a mudlark again, struggling in the slime on the banks of the Thames; the more he struggled the quicker he was held and the deeper he sank. The Nightmare Child's eyes sucked him in until he was swallowed completely.

Ben blinked beneath the agonizing weight of that stare and when he opened his eyes again he was confused to find himself back at St Paul's, face-to-face with Mother Shepherd. "Benjamin," she said softly. "I've been so terribly worried about you."

The old woman gave an unnatural smile then, and Ben

looked disconcertedly at the corners of her mouth. Each movement of her lips caused tiny hairline fractures to splinter through skin as fine as plaster.

"But...I...you..." Ben spluttered.

"Yes, Benjamin, that's right," said Mother Shepherd, stretching her arms towards him for an embrace, "you *did* kill me." Her smile grew wider as Ben watched. Wider than any human smile could stretch, splitting at the sides until it stretched to her ears, showing every tooth in her mouth from front to back.

"No, but, I didn't...it was an accident." Ben stumbled over his words as he struggled to move away from her, his arms throbbing with pain as the ropes bit deep. "I...I..."

"Killed me," she completed. "I always knew that you would. You nasty, hateful child."

"But you said you believed in me," Ben protested.

"How could I believe in you?" Her voice was filled with scorn as the spider's web of cracks spread to cover her face. "You're just an ignorant urchin from the gutter. You don't even believe in yourself!" Huge chunks of her head began to crumble away then, reminding Ben of the stone balustrade that had caused her death.

"You were *never* going to be the Hand of Heaven, Benjamin, *never*! The Uncreated One doesn't give that sort of power to boys like you. Don't you know that He hates boys who kill their mothers?"

Ben's blood ran cold.

He closed his eyes, and this time when he dared to open them again he discovered that Mother Shepherd had gone and he was looking at a much younger woman. A woman who he had never seen with his own eyes but had loved in his heart for the whole of his life.

"Ma," said Ben, his heart breaking. "Is it really you?"

The woman turned to face him completely, her red-gold hair brushing Ben's skin with the smell of sunshine. "My son," she said, cupping his face in her hands. "My precious Ben."

"Yes, Ma, it's me."

"Why did you kill me, Ben?"

Ben felt despairingly afraid. Defenceless. Hopeless. Defeated.

He screwed his eyes shut, putting all his remaining strength into keeping them closed. His mother was standing in front of him. *His dead mother*. Smiling and calling him a murderer. If he saw the look on her face one more time, it would break him, mind and soul.

I must not open my eyes. I must not open my eyes. I must not open my eyes.

"Ben!"

He opened his eyes.

"*Ben!*"

Lucy couldn't stand by and watch.

It had been easy enough for her to sneak into the Feast with Ghost and Jago Moon. All they had to do was wear the hoods that Hans had smuggled out for them and blacken their faces so they could mingle with the crowd. But now that they were on the inside and the gates had been locked, Lucy felt threatened on every side.

"I'm going to get him," she said.

"No," Moon warned. "You're not." He grabbed her arm and held her back. "Stick to the plan."

On the platform, Ben dangled like a puppet, convulsed with inner torment.

"Hold on, Ben!" Lucy shouted above the jeering crowd, breaking free from Moon's grip. "I'm coming!"

"Here we go again," Jago Moon muttered, reaching for his swordstick and following her into the fray.

"*Ben!*"

Lucy kept shouting his name, trying to be heard above the crowd. She barged her way through to the front, then made a sprint for the platform. But as she drew nearer to the baleful presence of the Nightmare Child, all of her strength seemed to melt away like wax.

Ben appeared to have fainted and the Nightmare Child was triumphant. Lucy took three more steps towards them and then the evil cherub snapped its head towards her. Lucy froze as it locked her in its stare.

"First your father, then your brother, and now Benjamin," purred the Nightmare Child. "You just can't look after your boys, can you, Lucy?"

Instinctively Lucy's fingers rushed to the scar that ran the length of her pretty face. The pain was so fresh that she thought her hand would come away bloody. Lucy wasn't in the Tower of London any more, she was back at *that* day, the worst day of her life. The day that haunted her in her darkest dreams.

There was a moment of horrific overlap, as reality and fantasy merged. In the dream world she saw a man's mouth, each one of his white teeth filed to a spiteful point. She knew his name, she knew that she had to get away from him, but he was getting nearer and nearer... In the real world she saw men dressed in ravens' feathers, looming at her, twisting and spinning insanely to the rhythmic beating of a drum...

Out of the corner of her eye she thought she could see Jago Moon, clasping his gnarled hands over his ears as he tried to shut out the Nightmare Child's whispers. Then Lucy's legs buckled and she tumbled to the ground, as all the phantoms of her past came to gloat.

You killed your mother, Ben. It's your fault she's dead.

All Ben's life there had been a wound inside him which had never fully healed, an old scab which bled every time he went back to pick at the memory. For a long time he had seen accusation on his father's face. For a long time Ben had been wrong.

But since Tower Bridge, Ben had no doubt that his father loved him – had *always* loved him. Jonas Kingdom didn't resent his son, he cherished him. *You're all I've got. You and your brother.*

So while the vision of his mother screamed abuse at him, Ben listened to his father's voice instead.

He was Ben Kingdom. He was the Hand of Heaven.

And he wasn't in the mood to listen to a pack of lies.

Ben looked at the Nightmare Child – not at any apparition that it had conjured up or at an image that it had sown in Ben's mind – but straight at *it*.

Ben's eyes actively sought the fallen angel's gaze and once he found it, he held it, unblinking. With quiet confidence Ben smiled at it – his biggest, brashest, cockiest grin – and in that fleeting instant he saw the Nightmare Child's pupils dilate with shock.

Its power was broken.

"Oi, sailor boy," Ben shouted at the Nightmare Child. "I've got a bone to pick with you."

It was like waking up. One moment Lucy was reliving the darkest day of her life, and the next she suddenly found herself lying on the damp grass, curled up like an infant.

The clammy fingers that had crawled inside her head had weakened. Something – someone – had broken the connection. It had to be Ben, she realized, as she saw him facing down the eerie child.

Lucy shook her head violently as if she could somehow dislodge the last of the thoughts that had invaded her mind. She slapped herself hard across the cheek. The grip was loosening, she realized. She struck herself again, even harder this time. And then Lucy was back.

Fully awake. Fully aware.

And really, really angry.

Drunken Legionnaires had began to gather around her. She nimbly flipped up from the floor and onto her feet in a graceful move. "Back off!" she roared in their faces, emphasizing her point by jabbing her staff deep into one man's belly. Most of them obliged, but one young Legionnaire stepped even closer.

"You want to dance, Scarface?" Bedlam leered.

"No," said Lucy, and without waiting for him to make his move she cracked him round the side of the skull with her staff. It made a very satisfying *thwack*. *Maybe it's because his head is hollow*, she thought with some satisfaction as she watched him slide unconscious to the ground.

The others quickly decided that she wasn't the sort of girl to mess with and they backed away. Turning, Lucy saw that Ben was engaged in some sort of stand-off with the Nightmare Child. She was only a few yards away from the platform now and she sprinted towards it, using her quarterstaff to vault up beside Ben. She was so relieved that he was still alive that Lucy surprised herself, and him, by planting a small hot kiss on his cheek. Then she drew her knife and slashed through Ben's bonds, sending him tumbling to the deck.

Lucy unclipped a spare quarterstaff from her belt. "You're going to need this," she said.

Ben's eyes held hers for a moment.

"Well, what are you waiting for?" she prompted.

CHAPTER 35

THE BATTLE
OF THE
BLOODY TOWER

Ben looked at the Nightmare Child and wondered what he had been afraid of. Now that the power of the fallen angel's lies had been broken, what was left for Ben to face? A small boy, dressed in a sailor's suit – with the sort of smug expression that was begging for a punch.

"I don't think we've been properly introduced," said Ben, walking purposefully towards it, flexing some feeling back into his hands. "My name is Ben Kingdom." His voice began to swell inside him. "I'm a Watcher! I'm the Hand of Heaven! And it's your turn to feel afraid!"

Ben rolled his right hand into a fist and swung a blow at the Nightmare Child's head, catching it with such force that the creature was lifted from its feet and sent sprawling to the deck. It took a second to recover before it scuttled backwards, crablike, hissing and spitting as it retreated.

Moon chose this moment to charge at Mr. Sweet with a growl. The first slash from his swordstick drew a line down Sweet's cheek, and the big man staggered back, snatching up a sabre to defend himself. Meanwhile, Ben and Lucy ran over to the cage where Nathaniel was being held and between them managed to wrench open the door. Nathaniel fell out onto the deck and Ben gently cradled his brother's head with his throbbing right hand.

At first, the eyes that gazed back at Ben were vacant and unknowing. "It's me," said Ben. "It's your brother." Then recognition dawned.

Nathaniel smiled. "I knew you'd come for me."

"Don't talk," Moon shouted. "Fight!"

Behind them, the Nightmare Child clambered back onto its feet, a thin trickle of blood escaping from the corner of its mouth. It clapped its tiny hands in amusement. "It's so much fun when you silly humans think there is hope. It makes it all the more delicious when you realize that there is none!"

Lucy and Ben supported Nathaniel's body between them but they were running out of options.

All around them, the Legion continued to bay and

cheer, enjoying the drama unfolding on the stage as if it were all part of the celebration. Meanwhile, the two huge Feathered Men on the platform both spread their black wings and launched a joint attack on Moon.

"This is all very touching," said Mr. Sweet, reaching inside the folds of his cloak, "but sometimes when you want something doing, you just have to do it yourself."

With that he pulled out a pistol, straightened his arm and levelled it at Ben.

"Goodnight, Ben Kingdom," he said with a sneer.

It was then that the crossbow bolt pierced Sweet's shoulder, sending his bullet high and wide.

Ben turned to see Ghost leaping up onto the platform beside them, another bolt ready, and a look of determination on his face. But this fight was far from over, Ben knew. There was danger on every side. A Feathered Man was screaming down towards Ghost, and the Nightmare Child was charging straight for Ben, its hands outstretched and hunting for his throat.

Ghost reacted with his usual silent proficiency, switching his aim from Sweet's chest and firing his bolt at the Feathered Man instead. At such close range the bolt went clean through the creature's head, stopping it dead. But Sweet used the distraction to retreat, reclaiming his fallen pistol and snapping off a shot. The bullet grazed

Ghost's leg and knocked him off his feet.

Meanwhile, Jago Moon had dispatched the first of the Feathered Men but didn't have a moment to regain his breath before he was rewarded with a ferocious attack from the remaining fallen angel. Moon ducked a slash that would have taken his head off, responded with a straight kick to the creature's stomach, and then skewered it with his sword cane.

The Nightmare Child cannonballed into Ben with surprising force, knocking Nathaniel from his arms. It slashed at Ben's face, raking sharp nails down his cheek.

"We can play this game if you prefer," it squealed.

Lucy swung her quarterstaff round in a strike that should have brought the fallen cherub down, but the creature ducked and turned on her with a snarl.

"Get them!" Sweet shouted to his drunken army as Moon charged towards him again. Sweet loosed off a shot, which Moon ducked, somehow sensing it coming. Two Legionnaires mounted the stage and Sweet lost no time placing himself safely behind them. "Don't just stand there, you imbeciles," he ordered, shoving them in Moon's direction.

In the crowd another figure responded instantly. Ben spotted Mickelwhite racing towards him, a thin streak of malice, with his sword raised.

"I'm looking forward to this!" Mickelwhite yelled, his blade glinting in the firelight.

He was nearly at the platform when Hans Schulman blundered into him clumsily, knocking them both to the ground in a sprawling heap. "I am so sorry, my Captain," Schulman spluttered. "Forgive me, I tripped in the dark."

"Idiot!" said Mickelwhite, looking at the German boy with contempt. "You ham-fisted oaf!"

Hans made to help his captain back onto his feet, but somehow he managed to slam his elbow into the side of Mickelwhite's head instead. "Whoops," said Hans with a secret smile, as Mickelwhite slumped unconscious back to the ground.

He had brought his Watcher friends a few seconds, but all around him the crowd was swarming towards the platform with a single purpose – to fight.

Ghost had used his last bolt and was wrestling on the ground with a man twice his size. Lucy was swinging her quarterstaff with amazing dexterity but she couldn't hold back the tide for ever. Jago Moon battled against a pair of brutish Legionnaires. A straight kick to the stomach folded one of them in half, while the other walked into a punch which flattened his nose.

Using his own men as a human shield, Sweet

snapped off another shot but the heaving of fighting bodies threw off his aim.

Overhead the night sky was swollen with clouds. The ravens and the Feathered Men were circling slowly and then Ben saw the flock suddenly shift, as if they had detected some danger in the air. It was probably just the blood throbbing in his ears, but Ben thought that he could hear a droning noise, like a swarm of approaching bees. It grew louder and louder.

Then he understood what it must be.

The humming was very close now but it wasn't insects, Ben knew. It had a steady *whump, whump, whump* rhythm which could only be made by an engine.

Ben saw Mr. Sweet's eyes grow wide with amazement and then shrink to slits of anger as he understood for the first time how badly he had underestimated the Watchers.

As the Liberator broke through the clouds overhead, Ben thought how magnificent it was – a battleship in the sky.

The hull was made of wood and brass. Big enough to hold twenty Watchers, it was carried through the air by a long, sleek bullet of silk, inflated with stolen gas. At the midpoint on each side, where the oars might have been on a conventional boat, there were steam-driven propellers.

The Liberator turned sharply and began a swooping

descent. Ben caught a glimpse of his father at the helm, holding the wheel and steering the airship as if he had been born to it. Josiah was there too, standing at the prow; a noble figurehead with sword drawn.

Rope ladders began to clatter down from the airship and Ben saw their chance. With a final desperate shove, he managed to push the Nightmare Child away and ran to his brother's side.

"Go!" said Ben. "Hurry!" he called to the other Watchers, who had put paid to the Legionnaires on the platform for now. "We won't get a second shot at this."

Nathaniel made an attempt to stand, but his legs wouldn't hold him and he fell to the deck. "Mr. Moon!" Ben called.

"Stop them!" Sweet bellowed.

Another group of Legionnaires started to mount the platform, just as a hail of crossbow bolts from the airship made them think twice. Sweet was quick enough to grab a Legionnaire and save himself from the missile that would have struck him.

"I can't think of a better cause to die for," said Sweet as the Legionnaire slumped in his arms.

Jago Moon had reached the foot of one of the rope ladders, with Nathaniel slung effortlessly over his shoulder; Ghost and Lucy weren't far behind. Ben saw one of the Watchers launch a missile at the Tower wall and it exploded with deafening force. Sweet flung himself to the ground and the Legionnaires cowered as a shower of sparks rained down. A wave of panic spread through the crowd.

Before the Legionnaires could recover from the shock, there was a second explosion, bigger and more destructive than the first.

Bombs!

Ben grinned. Even now, the Watchers stayed true to their Creed. He could see that each bomb was targeted to land on the stonework of the Tower, *not* on the Legion – they were meant to spread confusion, not cause death. It was an effective tactic, Ben thought, as he watched the Legionnaires begin to stampede for the gates like startled cattle.

One Legionnaire was running in the opposite direction though, heading directly for the rope ladders. Ben barely recognized Alexander Valentine – he looked so full of life since the Hand of Heaven had touched him.

"Take me with you!" he begged. "Please!"

Ben rushed to his side and helped the boy up onto the first rungs, which swayed alarmingly. "You'll get used to it," said Ben. "Welcome to the Watchers."

The Liberator began to lift higher, and Ben clambered onto the ladder behind him.

They were ten feet off the ground, and rising, when Ben felt cold fingers grasp him around the ankles. He looked down into the face of the Nightmare Child. The spiteful creature opened its mouth and sank its teeth into Ben's leg, making him howl with pain.

Ben did his best to kick the creature off but the fallen cherub was as tenacious as it was vicious – it scratched and clawed and bit at Ben, doing everything that it could to make him fall.

There came a loud *crack!* and Ben felt a bullet sing past his head. Looking down, he saw Mr. Sweet standing in the middle of the chaos, aiming his gun right at Ben, the Crown of Corruption on his head. At his feet was the pathetic figure of Claw Carter, watching forlornly as the airship rose steadily upwards. The Tower of London was ablaze around them, turning the clouds above the colours of blood and fire.

Another *crack!* Another whisper of death, even closer than the first.

Crossbow bolts hit the platform at Sweet's feet, but the man didn't even flinch. The Nightmare Child slackened his grip, only to bite Ben again with renewed ferocity. Ben looped his arm through the rope ladder to get a better grip and did everything he could to shake the beast off. And all the while the heat from the fire beneath them grew in intensity. Sweat rolled from Ben's brow. Sparks landed on him, filling his nostrils with the tang of singed cloth and burning hair.

Just then the Liberator gave a lurch, obviously struggling to lift higher above the flames. Then Ben realized Sweet hadn't missed – he'd been aiming for the balloon. Now the Feathered Men, who'd been circling, suddenly shrieked and swooped towards the airship. A volley of crossbow bolts sang out from the Liberator, perforating wings, piercing the enemy. But still the Feathered Men came, screeching all the louder.

Lucy leaned over the side of the ship. "The Hand," she called down. "Use the Hand."

And suddenly Ben knew exactly what he should do.

All of his thoughts came together with absolute clarity. He still felt the pain in his skin and the heat of the flames as the Tower of London burned. He still saw the Nightmare Child and Mr. Sweet, both wishing him death. And yet Ben felt only deep calm.

He smiled up at Lucy as he felt the raw energy begin to surge through his right hand. Then he wrapped both arms tightly around the Nightmare Child and together they dropped like a stone.

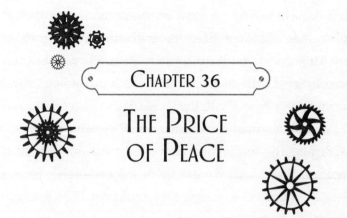

CHAPTER 36

THE PRICE
OF PEACE

Ben and the Nightmare Child fell together, turning in the air, until they hit the stage with a bone-rattling crunch. All the air left Ben's lungs in a sudden rush, leaving him totally winded. It must have been even worse for the Nightmare Child, he imagined; the cherub had broken their fall. Ben climbed off the tiny form, the power continuing to build in his right hand and arm.

Ben rose shakily to his feet just as the Nightmare Child's eyes snapped open again. The foul creature began to hiss and mutter an incantation under its breath. Ben didn't recognize the angry chattering language, but he could hear the spite behind the words. Unable to accept defeat, its jibbering rose to a crescendo until it seemed fit to explode, the rage inside its miniature frame growing too huge for its body to contain. Before Ben's eyes, the Nightmare Child dispersed into a cloud of fog. For a second Ben was left with the image of its vengeful lips and the sound of a final curse, and then, they too were gone.

Ben heard the clicking of an empty gun and turned to face Mr. Sweet. All around them the fire raged. Flames licked hungrily at whatever they could find. The heat was incredible, an oppressive wall that hemmed Ben in on all sides. It was always going to come down to this, Ben understood, as he faced Mr. Sweet alone.

Because the Watchers had been so careful with their aim, the wooden stage hadn't suffered a direct hit by the bombs, but it was burning around the edges and the flames were gaining in strength by the second. Ben, Sweet and Carter were stranded like three castaways on a raft, adrift on the waves of a burning sea. Clouds of embers filled the air around them, and Ben had to push through the wall of heat. He took another pace towards Mr. Sweet...and it was Mr. Sweet who took a step back, kicking Carter out from under his feet.

"Stay where you are, Kingdom!"

Sweet's voice was loud, but Ben could make out the cracks that were starting to appear in the man's colossal self-confidence. Ben rolled up his sleeve and pointed his arm like a weapon. "You know what this is, don't you?" Ben challenged. "This is your chance to run home like a good boy."

Ben could feel the naked electricity leaping invisibly between the outstretched fingers of his right hand and he stepped forwards again. This was the power that had brought down a storm of hailstones which smashed the Feathered Men from the sky. What would happen if all that force was unleashed against a single man?

Sweet took another slow step back, reaching for a fallen sword. The planks beneath them shuddered as the posts which supported them began to give way to the inferno. Ben could feel the soles of his skyboots beginning to burn as the fire ate away at the platform itself.

"I've never run from anything in my life," said Mr. Sweet, "and I'm not going to start today."

In the same instant, one side of the platform collapsed, sending Mr. Sweet staggering. Sweet muttered a foul oath as he stumbled. Then he swore again, louder and uglier, when he saw that he had strayed too near the flames.

It happened too quickly for either him or Ben to react.

The hem of Sweet's magnificent feathered cloak brushed against the flames and there followed a long agonizing second when Sweet knew what was coming and understood that he was powerless to prevent it. The flames soared up his body, claiming him from head to foot. Ben could do nothing, except pity the man's agony, as Mr. Sweet lurched away, to be instantly swallowed by the thick fog of the black smoke, leaving only his screams and the stench of burning feathers to remember him by.

"Now," said Ben, standing over the helpless form of Claw Carter. "Let's finish this."

Claw Carter, enemy of the Watchers, looked up at Ben. A long string of drool escaped from the corner of the professor's mouth.

Ben placed the Hand of Heaven on the professor's head and felt its energy flow from him. They were surrounded by fire, but none of it burned as brightly as the fire which passed through Ben now.

"Come back," said Ben with quiet authority. "Come back, Professor James Carter."

Carter began to shudder. Violent convulsions sent his arms and legs into spasm. Still Ben spoke over him, not relinquishing his grip. "This isn't how it ends for you," said Ben.

With that, Claw Carter went limp and collapsed. For a second, Ben wondered whether the power of the Hand had destroyed Carter completely. He gazed down at Carter's face, looking for signs of life.

Carter's eyes opened with a start, as if he had woken from a deep and terrible sleep and no longer understood the world around him.

"Do you know who I am?" said Ben, crouching down and searching his eyes for a flicker of recognition.

"Yes, I know you," said Carter, raising his claw. "You're Ben Kingdom."

"That I am," said Ben, with a touch to his billycock. "And do you know what my most powerful weapon is?"

Carter hesitated.

"Forgiveness," said Ben.

Carter froze, then lowered his claw and put his human hand on Ben's shoulder in the affectionate way he used to do, way back before Ben knew anything of the Legion or the Watchers. Back when Ben was just a mudlark, bringing his treasures to the brilliant professor who lived in the basement of the British Museum.

"I don't understand what you've done to me," said Carter. "Or why—"

"You're a clever bloke," said Ben. "You'll work it out."

Claw Carter rose unsteadily to his feet, surveying the scene of desolation around them. The fire was drawing closer. Ben spun, searching for a way through the inferno but even as he did so the flames leaped higher, driven by the draught of giant wings. Talons pierced Ben's shoulders and he was plucked off the ground. Three Fingers had returned.

Ben's legs flailed as Three Fingers drew him higher. Ben had lost his quarterstaff, leaving him with nothing but his bare hands to try to defeat the creature. It was never going to be enough.

"Carter!" Ben cried out, searching for the professor even as the Feathered Man dragged him into the air. Smoke stung Ben's eyes and he lost sight of Carter in the flames; surely it couldn't finish like this?

The Liberator was hovering, but Ben could see the Watchers had their own fight on their hands, trying to keep the airship steady in the updraught from the flames and simultaneously repel the Feathered Men that were circling around it.

Then came the flash of white, and the sound of mighty wings, as Josiah swooped in. Ben's heart soared as the Weeping Man flew towards him, sword in hand. Above him, Three Fingers hissed in anger and alarm.

"Release him," Josiah demanded, "and I can let you depart in peace."

Three Fingers shrieked and snapped his beak in defiance, holding Ben with one hand so that he could slash out with the other. Josiah dodged the blow and came in beneath it, pushing his sword into the Feathered Man's side. With a gurgle, Three Fingers went limp and began to fall, releasing his grasp on Ben. Ben was left hanging in empty space, but before he could tumble to his death, Josiah caught him in both arms.

With a combination of harpoons, crossbows and sheer determination, the Watchers had managed to fend off the Feathered Men, but their victory would be short-lived if they didn't make good their escape soon. As Josiah reached the side of the Liberator, three pairs of hands stretched out to haul Ben over the side: Jonas, Lucy and Ghost. Ben could see Jago Moon tending to Nathaniel.

They had made it.

Ben turned to smile at Josiah. Then the expression on the Weeping Man's face changed, suddenly and terribly.

A spot of crimson emerged in the centre of his white shirt. Followed by the tip of a sword, which had pierced his body.

Wounded and bloody, Three Fingers had flown up behind them and, in a single move, snatched Josiah's sword from its sheath and plunged it into the Weeping Man's back.

"Noooo!" shouted Ben. Lucy whipped up her crossbow pistol and fired at the leering Feathered Man. Then came a frozen moment: something exploded in the Tower beneath them, sending up a huge blossom of fire, which rocked the Liberator from prow to stern. Three Fingers and Josiah were suspended in the air. And then they both fell down into the flames.

Ben grasped at empty air as his friend disappeared into the smoke. Simultaneously a black cloud began to rise in the distance: a fresh swarm of Feathered Men emerging from the Under.

"Ben! We have to go," said Jonas Kingdom, taking the wheel and opening the Liberator up to full throttle.

Ben slumped to the deck, more exhausted than he had ever been, while the airship lifted them higher and higher into the bruised and angry sky.

EPILOGUE

15TH MARCH, 1892

Night gave way to a cold, crisp day. The fog had departed with the Nightmare Child, but the London it left behind was tattered and torn. Ben stood with a small band of Watchers on the roof of Lancaster House, looking out on Buckingham Palace. Jago Moon had led them there. Ghost was there too, with his leg bandaged, and Valentine and Jonas Kingdom and Nathaniel. Lucy was standing beside Ben and he reached for her hand as they waited for the dawn, each of them lost in their own thoughts.

The sun when it came was weak and feeble, yet they all bathed in its glow, relieved that they could feel its embrace again. Ben felt his hopes rise with the sun.

None of them had spoken much since the battle of the Bloody Tower.

Mother Shepherd was gone.

Josiah was gone.

But the Watchers would live on.

Ben realized that he was still wearing the silk scarf that Ruby Johnson had given him and he tugged it loose. After staring at it for a second, he pitched it over the side of the building and it fluttered to the ground.

"Why did you do that?" asked Lucy.

"It didn't suit me," said Ben, adjusting his billycock.

Lucy looked as if she was about to say something but a disturbance at the palace drew their eyes. A swarm of figures surged into the courtyard, but they weren't dressed in the brilliant red of the Household Guards. They wore the black feathers of the Legion.

The Legionnaires fell silent as the doors opened on the palace balcony and a figure strode into view. His hands were bandaged and half of his face was livid red from the kiss of the flames. But on his head was a crown, made from thirty silver coins.

Ben felt as if he had been punched in the stomach. Sweet was alive and the Crown of Corruption was his.

"Uncreated One, have mercy," Lucy breathed.

Mr. Sweet waited for silence and then clenched his fist to his chest in the Legion salute. "All hail your new King!" Mr. Sweet commanded.

Moon grimaced as he heard Sweet's voice and the rapturous cheers of the crowd.

The red, white and blue of the Union flag was lowered and in its place a new standard was hoisted: the clenched fist of the Legion.

"This is a new day!" shouted Mr. Sweet, as first one, then a dozen Feathered Men began to lift themselves into the air from their roost on the roof of Buckingham Palace.

"Yes," said Ben, turning his back on Mr. Sweet and facing the Watchers. "It is a new day, for the Watchers too. Mother Shepherd isn't with us, Josiah isn't with us, but I stand here as your leader, if you'll have me."

"We trust you, Ben," said Lucy.

"Thank you," said Ben, from his heart. "Trust me on this then… I'd like you to meet my first recruit."

A man climbed up the rope ladder and joined them on the roof. A tall man with a weather-beaten face and a claw for a hand.

For an empty second no one said a word.

"I know those footsteps," growled Jago Moon.

"Claw Carter," Lucy gasped.

"No need for introductions then," said Ben. "Come on," he said, leading the Watchers away. "We've got work to do."

BEN'S ADVENTURES CONTINUE IN 2014.
TURN THE PAGE FOR A SNEAK PREVIEW
OF HIS NEXT BATTLE...

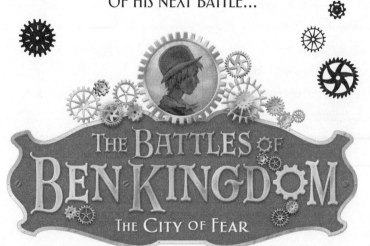

THE BATTLES OF
BEN KINGDOM
THE CITY OF FEAR

"So you think this will work?" whispered Ben, his back pressed against the wall, the rain making rivers down his face. Claw Carter ran his hand across his unshaven chin thoughtfully. The professor was tired, Ben thought, worn down to the bone; Mr. Sweet's reign of terror was taking a heavy toll on them all.

"It might, Ben," said Carter. "It just might." There was a distant expression in Carter's eyes as he spoke and once again, Ben realized quite how little he really knew about the man he had put his trust in.

"Then we have to do it," said Ben. "What other choice do we have?"

A fork of lightning rent the sky and for a brief moment Carter's wolfish face was illuminated. Ben was shocked by what he saw – the raw hunger of a predator. For all his words, Carter was still a dangerous man.

The stamp of heavy boots alerted them both to the brigade of Legionnaires approaching, hunting for curfew breakers – like them. Ben pushed himself into the shadows of the side alley, Carter beside him. Keep your head down, Benny boy. If they escaped the patrol there was still a chance that they could get to the palace...where their troubles would really begin.

Ben felt Carter's hand land firmly on his shoulder and give a squeeze of reassurance. A cannonade of thunder rolled across the city, shaking windows in its fury. The Legionnaires were level with the alleyway now, their own heads tucked against their chests as the rain lashed down.

They aren't going to spot us, *thought Ben with relief.*

"Here!" shouted Carter, leaping to his feet. "Over here!"

"What are you doing?" gasped Ben as the Legionnaires swivelled, their rifles raised.

Carter kept his grip on Ben and shoved him into the open, his claw now resting on Ben's throat.

"Claw Carter!" snarled the captain, not lowering his gun.

"The very same."

"You know what we do to traitors."

"I do, but I'm no traitor," Carter smiled. "I'm the man who brings Ben Kingdom's head on a plate."

TO FIND OUT WHAT HAPPENS NEXT, LOOK OUT FOR

COMING IN 2014

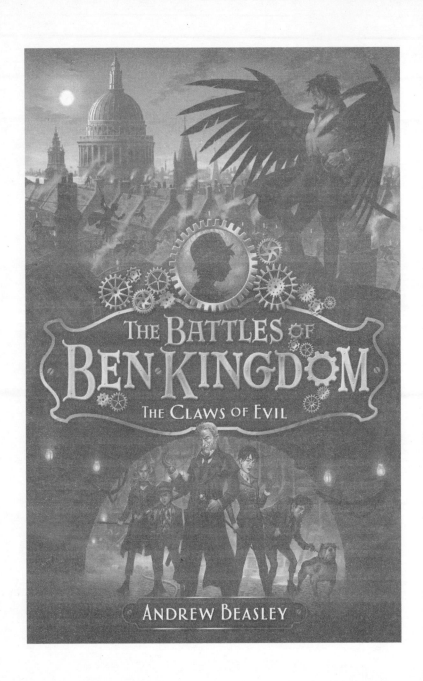

CATCH UP WITH BEN'S FIRST BATTLE IN

THE CLAWS OF EVIL

EVERY COIN HAS TWO FACES,
EVERY WAR HAS TWO SIDES.
ONE BOY HAS TO MAKE THE RIGHT CHOICE.

The year is 1891, and LONDON is at war. High up on the
rooftops lives a ragtag band of orphans and spies – the
WATCHERS – PROTECTORS of the city. But below the
cobbled streets lurks the LEGION, a ruthless gang of
CUT-THROATS and thieves, plotting to unleash the
darkest forces of HELL.

When a MYSTERIOUS coin falls into his hands, cocky
street urchin, BEN KINGDOM, is flung into the midst of
this ancient BATTLE. The fate of the world rests with
Ben, but which side will he choose? An army of angels...
or THE CLAWS OF EVIL.

ISBN: 9781409544005
EPUB: 9781409557258   KINDLE: 9781409557265

BEN's GUIDE TO LONDON WATCHER SLANG

AN UNORTHODOX GLOSSARY FOR SOME OF THE MORE
UNUSUAL WORDS, WEAPONS AND PHRASES TO BE
FOUND IN THIS BOOK.

ballyhoo: uproar, noise, an ear-splitting racket. A most common sound to be heard on the streets of London now the Legion are at large.

billycock: a felt hat with a low, rounded crown, like a bowler. The best sort of hat there is, and I'm so pleased I've got another one!

billystick: a short club, made of wood or metal, used in the fight against Sweet and his minions. Also comes in handy when rescuing people trapped in fires, fogs and other predicaments if you need to smash a window or break down a door. Sometimes know as a **cosh**.

bolas: a throwing weapon made of weights placed at the end of interconnected lengths of cord. Favoured by Jago Moon, this is particularly excellent for sweeping those rotten Legionnaires off their feet.

brainpan: the skull-shaped bone what holds your head (or **bonce**) in. Worth looking after, if I were you.

brass it out: what you say to yourself when faced with a task that appears frightening, unpleasant or difficult. Take a deep breath, be brave, and *brass it out*!

chandler: a dealer in supplies for all things nautical. As ships and boats are always in need of rope, these places are an excellent Watcher resource.

costermonger: a noisy street trader of fruit, veg, fish or other goods who sells straight from a handcart.

cut up rusty: to flex your muscles and start a fight. What you do when faced with the likes of Grey Wing, Mickelwhite, Bedlam and Dips.

every man Jack: you, me, the bloke next door, the Watcher on the roof and the Legion in the gutter – basically every single person you can think of.

eyrie: the nest of a hawk, eagle or other bird of prey, as well as the camp and lookout of a Watcher.

garibaldi biscuit: a specialty of Peek, Frean and Co biscuit manufacturers, consisting of two thin crispy biscuits with currants jammed between them so it looks like a squashed-fly sandwich. Named after Italian general, Giuseppe Garibaldi, who visited the north of England in 1861.

Huzzah!: What toffs say when there's something worth celebrating.

iron maiden: a most gruesome and cruel instrument of torture, this coffin-shaped box is littered with iron spikes, designed to hurt the miserable wretch imprisoned inside should they fidget.

Knightsbridge: a very fashionable and well-to-do area of West London, and therefore a prime location for stopping no-good Legionnaire cutpurses and pickpockets.

knuckleduster: a metal guard worn over the knuckles to increase the impact of a punch when engaged in hand-to-hand combat with a Legionnaire. Nasty, but effective.

lucifer: a match (but also one of the many names that old beast, the Devil, goes by).

Metropolitan line: the world's first underground railway service, and a fast-track exit out of the Under. Carriage-riding not for the faint-hearted.

mudlark: someone, usually an underappreciated boy, who makes a living scavenging in river mud for items of value. It does mean you get to keep the richest pickings for yourself though.

mutton-chop whiskers: great big bushy hair on a fellow's cheek which resembles a juicy meat chop, being narrow at the top and rounded at the bottom. Perhaps I'll grow my own one day...

old Nichol: London's most notorious slum. Situated in the East End, it's a miserable place – filthy, overcrowded and desperately poor. Many young Watchers began life here before being brought to the rooftops.

ormolu: a very expensive way of making things look posh, which involves applying finely ground gold onto a bronze object using mercury. Although it looks nice, mercury don't half give off some evil fumes, so most ormolu gilders kick the bucket by the time they're forty. Still, makes a nice clock.

quarterstaff: a shaft of hardwood measuring several feet used for fighting and defence against the Legion. Collapsible variations are preferable, as these can be shortened, both to conceal the weapon, and to increase Watchers' speed and dexterity when running across rooftops.

swordstick: a hollow walking stalk, concealing a blade which can be used as a sword in the event of enemy attack.

Yeoman Warders: guardians of the Tower of London, tasked with the job of keeping an eye on the prisoners to ensure they don't escape, and the Crown Jewels to ensure nobody walks off with them.

Acknowledgements

A lot of midnight oil has gone into this book, and I never would have been able to write it without the encouragement, support and love of some incredible people.

I couldn't ask for a more caring or wise agent than the wonderful Anne Finnis. Thank you, Anne, for everything that you do – you're stuck with me for the long haul! Special thanks to the dynamic Caroline Hill-Trevor; I know that Ben Kingdom couldn't be in better hands. I also want to thank my friend Libby Allman and the team at Waterstones, Plymouth, for my amazing launch – I will treasure those memories for ever.

I want to thank the Federation of Children's Book Groups, especially the Plymouth gang, for their support, and the children and staff at Stoke Damerel Primary for sharing in my excitement. Special mention also has to go to Helen Greathead, whose talent and kindness opened the door for me in the first place.

I couldn't have found a better publisher than Usborne, and my list of lovely Usborne people is growing every day! Thanks, first of all, to Rebecca Hill, for her unstinting support and enthusiasm for these books. Thanks to Amy Dobson for organizing my incredible tour, and to Anna Howorth and Carolyn Koussa for making it such a joyful experience. I'm thrilled every time I go into a bookshop and find my book, and I know that it is you guys I have to thank for getting it there.

The *Ben Kingdom* books have an established style now and it still takes my breath away. Thanks to Hannah Cobley for her incredible, eye-catching design and Ian McNee for the dramatic map. Each time the book jumps off the shelf, you can take the credit. Special thanks belong to David Wyatt. I didn't know how he would ever top the cover to book one, until I saw the cover of book two.

Very special thanks to my brilliant and talented editor, Stephanie King. Thank you, Stephanie, for caring about these stories as much as I do. Without your insight, this book wouldn't be half as good. Oh, and Constable Wilde forgives you for cutting all his scenes – again!

My family bring me endless joy and I could fill a book trying to describe my love for them. Trè and Christina, my American brother and sister, I love you guys across the miles. Mum and Jack, thank you for believing in me and sharing the adventure. Darling Amanda, I'll see you later, sis – save me a good seat. Mum and Dad, your generosity, your kindness and your limitless love mean everything to me. Ben and Lucy, being your dad is the best thing in the world. Already you are both so amazing and incredible, and we've hardly got going yet! My gorgeous Jules, you love me so much that you let me put 'author' on our wedding certificate almost a decade before I got published. This book would never have happened without you – my best friend, always and for ever.

And to the one who lights my path. *I love you all.*

ABOUT THE AUTHOR

ANDREW BEASLEY was born in Hertfordshire, and has spent most of his life with his nose buried in a book.

As a student he read law in Bristol, but was disappointed to discover that life as a lawyer wasn't as exciting as books had led him to believe. He then spent a number of years travelling extensively across Europe for work, although he didn't see much of it because he was usually reading a book.

Andrew is now a primary school teacher, where he shares his passion for storytelling with his class. Andrew lives in Cornwall with his wife and their two children, Ben and Lucy.

THE BATTLES CONTINUE AT
WWW.BENKINGDOM.COM